Reviews of Writings for a Car Boot Sale

◇◇◇

This book is a marvellous 'omnium gatherum' of pieces from a talented writer whose interests range wide. A campaigning and passionate dietitian, she writes with great authority on public health issues. The science is presented in an accessible and logical way, enthusing the reader with the same fervour to put things right. For a relaxing change of pace and feel, you can dip into one of her intriguing and cleverly constructed short stories, each thought provoking and highly entertaining. Change gear again and the author's original research shines new light on some notable pieces of 19th century English porcelain and an intriguing connection to Jane Austen. This unusual book provides variety like no other, its disparate topics linked by the author's lively and enquiring mind and sense of fun.

Fergus Gambon, Director of British Ceramics at Bonhams. He has made many appearances on BBC's Antiques Roadshow.

Here is a book which shows the mark of a writer who knows her business. It spans different genres – creative fiction, mystery and the academic – but the competence in each is clearly evident. Part One is particularly striking for the originality of language. Concision is combined with a deftness of touch which makes the reading challenging but rewarding. Such is the subtext that the short sketches bear multiple reading in order to appreciate the artistry. The result is a miscellany of felicitous phrasing that contrasts with the intriguing ceramic mysteries in Part Two and the scientific whistle-blowing in Part Three. Put the parts together and you have an author who has talent in fields not normally found within the same volume. It's quite an achievement.

John Dougill, author of many books, often with a focus on the literary and cultural history of places. He taught English in Oxford, before settling in Kyoto: Professor Emeritus of British Studies at Ryukoku University, Kyoto.

Intriguing glimpses into the chequered history of ceramics are sandwiched between a fine collection of short stories and a voyage of discovery in plain English into the controversy surrounding the widespread use of artificial sweeteners. *Writings for a Car Boot Sale* lives up to its title in being well worth a rummage.

> **Maggie Cobbett, Yorkshire writer of fiction, features and poetry. Her books reflect this variety and include novels and a guide to crafting lucrative fillers.**

Other books by the author of *Writings for a Car Boot Sale*:

Corkscrewed, P. Theophilus. Novel. ISBN 978-1783064-724 Pub. Matador, imprint of Troubador Publishing Ltd. 2014

Billingsley, Brampton and Beyond; In search of The Weston Connection. Pamela (Theophilus) Gardner. Non-fiction. ISBN 978-1848763-470 Pub. Matador, imprint of Troubador Publishing Ltd. 2010

Writings for a Car Boot Sale

Take the Box

Pamela Theophilus Gardner

Copyright © 2020 Pamela Theophilus Gardner

The moral right of the author has been asserted.

Apart from any fair dealing for the purposes of research or private study, or criticism or review, as permitted under the Copyright, Designs and Patents Act 1988, this publication may only be reproduced, stored or transmitted, in any form or by any means, with the prior permission in writing of the publishers, or in the case of reprographic reproduction in accordance with the terms of licences issued by the Copyright Licensing Agency. Enquiries concerning reproduction outside those terms should be sent to the publishers.

Matador
9 Priory Business Park,
Wistow Road, Kibworth Beauchamp,
Leicestershire. LE8 0RX
Tel: 0116 279 2299
Email: books@troubador.co.uk
Web: www.troubador.co.uk/matador
Twitter: @matadorbooks

ISBN 978 1838592 448

British Library Cataloguing in Publication Data.
A catalogue record for this book is available from the British Library.

Printed and bound in the UK by TJ International, Padstow, Cornwall
Typeset in 11pt Sabon by Troubador Publishing Ltd, Leicester, UK

Matador is an imprint of Troubador Publishing Ltd

Contents

◇◇◇

List of Illustrations	vii
Writings for a Car Boot Sale	1
Aunty Nora's Knowledge	2
Today's News	7
Essence of Albert Alexander	10
You and Me Both	22
Out of Sync	26
Today is History	33
New Riches	34
A Tale out of School	38
At the Centre	43
Independence Day	48
Untitled	51
Billingsley Roses	54
Introduction to Group II	77
The Mystery of Thomas Mason	81
Have You Seen This Woman?	90
Thurot vs. Tito	100
Was Miriam Weston of Sound Mind?	112
Introduction to Group III	127
Ponceau 4R. Its use in food & implications in allergy	131
Appendices to Ponceau 4R	146
The Insidious and Pernicious Promotion of Sweeteners is well orchestrated: Who is the Conductor?	152
No Ifs, Ands, or Buts	179

List of Illustrations

◇◇◇

The Mystery of Thomas Mason — 81
Figure 1. Minton vase, signed T. Mason
Figure 2. T. Mason signature
Figure 3. Mintons globe, in gold
Figure 4. Entries from Christie's Auction Catalogue

Have You Seen This Woman? — 90
Figure 1. Portrait on a porcelain can
Figure 2. Plate decorated by Julia Leigh
Figure 3. Plate decorated by Caroline Leigh
Figure 4. Daylesford House by Anne Rushout
Figure 5. Susannah Smith by James Leakey. Courtesy of Bonhams, UK
Figure 6. A close-up of the portrait on the can
Figure 7. A close-up of James Leakey's portrait of Susannah Smith
Figure 8. Bersted Lodge by Anne Rushout

Thurot vs. Tito — 100
Figure 1. Sèvres vase. Courtesy of Christie's, New York
Figure 2. Scene on the Sèvres vase
Figure 3. Creamware saucer
Figure 4. Scene on the creamware saucer
Figure 5. Vestigia delle Terme di Tito e loro Interne Pitture
Figure 6. Three figures near the stone bearing the picture's title
Figure 7. Engraving of a Smuglewicz picture
Figure 8. Tunnel entrance under Carrickfergus Castle

Figure 9.	The Great Hall, Carrickfergus Castle. Courtesy of 'The Carrick Times'	
Figure 10.	North Gate Entrance to Carrickfergus	

Was Miriam Weston of Sound Mind?   **112**

Figure 1.	Weston and Austen Connections (this and figure 2 are taken from the book 'Billingsley, Brampton and Beyond: In search of The Weston Connection')
Figure 2.	Miriam Weston's family
Figure 3.	'The Momentous Interview' by H.K. Browne
Figure 4.	'In Conference' by H.K. Browne
Figure 5.	'Bearer of Evil Tidings' by H.K. Browne

Ponceau 4R. Its use in food & implications in allergy   **131**

Appendix I.	Chemical Structure of Ponceau 4R
Appendix II.	Summary Table of Intakes of Colours
Appendix III.	Average diet/average level of use
Appendix IV.	Average diet/maximum level of use
Appendix V.	Extreme diet
Appendix VI.	Child's diet

The Insidious & Pernicious Promotion
of Sweeteners is well orchestrated: **152**
Who is the Conductor?
Cover image from the published essay

Writings for a Car Boot Sale

◇◇◇

In the corner lies a half-discarded heap, in need of a sort.

The charity bag says no bric-a-brac, no books; auction houses want better; eBay is not an option – nothing warrants the postage.

But everything has a worth to someone, somewhere.

A car boot sale is the answer. Guaranteed to draw that one canny individual to whom a sheltered, unrecognized, 'also comes with' item will appeal.

The rising heap is a collection of miscellany: essays; sketches; stories, tall and true: grown ever more diversified; a mixture that has no market, is themeless; homeless.

Think it. Write it. Put it in the box.

Booters rummage.

"A penny for this one" is offered. Take the box.

Aunty Nora's knowledge

◇◇◇

"Ambulance please, to the first allotment off Barker Field Lane … I don't know, I had to get back home to phone; I don't have a mobile. … Of course …"

Nora gave her name and contact details.

"Aunty Nora, will Mummy know where I am?" Molly asked. Nora reassured Molly that her mummy would surely realize where they were. But, she would take her home if Mummy hadn't collected her by six o'clock.

"Will Daddy be back from the hospital by then? … Why was his tummy hurting so much?"

Nora gave herself a little thinking time. "My, you do ask a lot of questions for a six-year old, don't you?" And turned away from the girl's searching eyes. "Let's see what we can find in this cupboard."

The ploy did not work.

"Aunty Nora, what's a peace-offering? Was the coffee you gave Daddy a peace-offering because the rose bush had died?"

"Oh Molly, I've no idea what you're talking about."

The words tumbled out, and Nora simultaneously encouraged books, board games, paper and pens to tumble out from their crammed store place: all manner of distractions for Molly. Molly honed in on the drawing pad. Nora frantically tried to piece together fragments of what Molly might have overheard.

The visit to the allotment had been purposeful. It had been planned but had it been wise to go through with the plan when Molly was also there? Had she been within earshot the whole time? Nora closed her eyes to shut out the present and to re recall detail of what had recently passed.

She re-lives her insinuation: goes over her opening attempt to get his attention and the precise progression to … what? She needs to be clear.

"I know what you're up to and you can pack it in. That rose bush was a mistake. I don't know about green fingers, I know yours are itchy and slimy."

He is nonplussed. She expands.

" 'Dream lover'. It disappears from your garden and one appears in the garden at number 46. On the very same day! The identical bush – the same shape; the same number of pink blooms; the same number of blooms turning to lilac; the same height – identical!"

He shows no emotion. She summarizes the inference, over-articulating each word. "Rose bush gone from your garden in the morning, in her garden by the afternoon."

"Is that right." He says.

She is infuriated by the tone; the words aren't posed as a question. Neither are they an acknowledgement of an interesting observation. It's a blatant put down. A 'think what you want, it doesn't matter, you're irrelevant' statement.

She draws in breath and pushes her point. "Yes, that *is* right. And that's a hell of a coincidence, don't you think?" But he gets worse.

"Hold the Press! One diseased rose bush is uprooted and another one is planted! ... Come off it Nora. Lame even for your imagination."

Such a mocking dismissal is not helping his case. She is sure of her ground and a denial will not be tolerated.

"We both know the significance of number 46; I've seen you sneaking in there. Think you're a 'dream lover' do you; think you're witty giving number 46 that bush? It was supposed to be a special anniversary gift for my sister: your wife. Hurt her again and I'll kill you."

Nora looked at Molly; tried to judge from her demeanour whether she had been privy to that particular part of the conversation. Molly was absorbed in drawing. Seemingly so, but not totally, as was demonstrated when she next spoke.

"Aunty Nora, was it a leafhopping pest that killed Mummy's special rose bush?"

Nora stalled. It was involuntary. Her thoughts were muddled still. "Leafhopper pest, Molly? Why do you say that?"

"Because when you said that to Daddy, he said you were very droll. Does droll mean right?"

The child's perceptions needed to be considered. Nora could not carry on stumbling and tripping up over explanations. Oh, what a mess!

Nora switched her thoughts. "Let's have a drink, shall we?"

Molly followed Nora into the kitchen and nodded her agreement as she trailed. She watched her aunty with an intensity that would have alarmed Nora, had she been aware.

"Do you have sugar in your coffee?" Molly asked. Nora replied that she did not.

"Do you sweeten it with a powder, like Mummy does?" was Molly's next question. Again, Nora replied that she did not.

Attention turned briefly to Molly and to what drink she would now choose to have. And then

"Aunty Nora, how do you know when there are too many leafhopping pests in the world?"

Nora mumbled her way through an exposition on how 'too many' or overpopulation was always relative to something else, such as food, space or, she supposed in this case, leaves.

No, that was not appropriate. It went no way near to answering what Molly wanted to know.

"But how do you know how much white powder to use when there are too many?"

Nora was flummoxed by that one. No idea at all. She knew nothing of how gardeners dealt with those or any other pests, she told Molly.

Molly was silenced. They took their drinks with them to the living room and Molly resumed her drawing. It was of a garden, to which she added a shape she described as a shed. With the drawing of the shed began Molly's running commentary:

"This is Daddy in the shed. This is you talking to Daddy … No; I'll draw you making the coffee. This is the shelf where Daddy keeps his gardening jars and here is the coffee, right at the end. … I'm glad I drew a big shed Aunty Nora. I'm filling all the space aren't I?"

Nora smiled towards her. The smile did not linger and Nora put down her mug with a look of discomfort.

"Aunty Nora, I've decided to draw you giving Daddy his mug of coffee. Daddy's saying 'I'm going to buy her another bush'. ... Is the bush for Mummy, Aunty Nora? ...

"Aunty Nora, Daddy doesn't like sugar in his coffee. And he doesn't like the sweetening powder either. Didn't you know that?"

"No, Molly. I did not know that."

Molly, once again, went silent. She soon stopped drawing, stood up and left the room, informing Nora, as she passed, that she was going to use the lavatory.

"Good girl." Nora said automatically, blandly: no expression on her face, no movement of her limbs.

The time Molly was out of the room did not register with Nora. It could have been minutes. It could have been hours. When Molly returned she knelt down by her drawing.

"Aunty Nora, do you think I should draw Daddy outside the shed, bending over because his stomach was hurting? I don't think I want to ...

"Did his stomach hurt because of the sweetening powder, Aunty Nora? You wouldn't have given him it if you'd known he didn't like it would you?"

Nora seemed not to hear.

Time passed.

"Aunty Nora, I think Mummy will be here soon. She said so. Shall I watch out for her?

"Mummy didn't know there was sweetening powder in the shed.

"Aunty Nora, come, quick! There's a police car. A policeman and a police lady have got out. Are they coming to see us? Why are they coming Aunty Nora?"

Nora told Molly that she could answer no more of her questions.

She gave a similar response to the police officers.

Today's News

◇◇◇

Tony: Can you be here early, to give Cleo a hand?

Marcus: Sorry. A misunderstanding. I wasn't planning on actually coming, but I will donate.

Tony: Oh, mate! Don't let me down. It would destroy Cleo; this charity is her lifeline. Others see the smiles; I see the suffering. Please! She needs my support and I need yours.

Marcus: But I couldn't do anything. And I've an appointment, this cataract's becoming …

Tony: I'm begging you mate. Come.

Marcus gave the open door a tap. He saw Tony cower under Cleo's glance as she turned to welcome her guest to "the 'Charity for Invisible Ills' event".

Cleo: So, Marcus. What are you?

The question surprised Marcus; he had met Tony through their similar work – which Cleo knew of, so why ask. Tony had already responded to Cleo's earlier glower and moved away to perform whatever duty was next expected, and, therefore, could not aid Marcus's understanding. Marcus answered directly.

"I'm a surveyor, I … "

Cleo: No, I mean what are you? This is it, you see. We can wear labels printed with our names and occupations but the labels of what we really are remain on the inside. I lost a sister and that hurt is deep-rooted.

Marcus: I'm terribly sorry. You must miss her.

Cleo: I do. I miss that I will never know her. She died two years before I was born. But enough about me, what are you … at the end of a spectrum, a 'free-from'…? We must talk about what we are.

Marcus: I am acutely aware of that, but I am nothing, just … alive.

She patted his arm and suggested he take some refreshment, comprising a glass of water. Cleo explained the catering situation.

"I cannot favour or discriminate between guests, and I'm expecting such a variety of 'free-froms' that no food or other drink is eligible."

Cleo left him in favour of new arrivals, and to put them in the picture.

Cleo: That's Marcus over there. He's suffering from acute awareness and low esteem. Only just alive!

The evening paper reported a man killed. He appeared to have simply not seen the car coming. "He must have been as blind as a bat, poor soul", a witness commented.

Essence of Albert Alexander

◇◇◇

"You'll never guess what I've come across", Andrew shouted to Isobel as he came through the back door.

Isobel determined not to show interest and mumbled "There's no point in my trying then, is there".

Her lack of enthusiasm was commonplace; Andrew carried on, undaunted.

"Can you remember when you were reading *Un Mauvais Rêve* by George Bernanos and you said you wished you could find an English translation?"

"I'm amazed you remembered the title."

He chose not to respond to either praise or ridicule of his memory, whichever had been intended. "The English translation is by Strachan and called *Night is Darkest*. I've bought it for you!"

Isobel looked about his person for sight of said book.

"It's in the car. Actually, it was one of a large box of books that …"

"I knew there'd be a catch", Isobel interrupted. "What was in the box that you wanted". The question was rhetorical.

"Unfair! It wasn't like that. I was passing *Back In Again* and saw they were unloading stuff from a house clearance – that widow's place this side of Leyburn."

"No idea what you're talking about."

" It has the huge oak tree, a bit too close to the house you said. ... And there ..."

"And the books?" Isobel asked. (Andrew seemed set to reminisce and she was not in the mood.)

"I think there are some good ones. We could sort through them and car boot or eBay those we don't want."

"You haven't said why you bought a box full, not just the novel for me."

This time Andrew came straight to the point. "Because you'd said an English translation of that particular Bernanos was rare; if I'd shown interest it might have drawn too much attention. I don't know the value of your book but there must be over fifty books in the box and I got the lot for thirty pounds! Got to be a bargain!"

(He did not see a necessity to make immediate mention of the few *Horses in Training* yearbooks he had spotted.)

The find was in August – the time of the Ebor meeting. Once their favourite racing meeting and venue, they had rarely given it a miss before Isobel's accident. Isobel had not been for ten years; Andrew had taken a four-year break but was now back on track, so to speak. He refused to acknowledge guilt for going, and invited Isobel in an exaggeratedly upbeat manner.

"The forecast is good. Do you fancy coming to York today

Issy? We could go in plenty of time before the first race and take some wine and a picnic."

Isobel declined, as always. "I think I'll make a start on sorting through those books while you're out."

Fear of the *Horses in Training* being discovered, so soon, was quickly supplanted by pleasure that at least Isobel was going to **do** something. And he had been the one to generate that interest. He was pleased.

"OK love. Should be fun. I can't wait to see what's in there! I wonder …" No need to make a big pretence of ignorance; he said no more.

(Andrew had learned to watch his words – he'd been careless in the past. He did not want his perceived impatience with her for 'not getting over it', for 'wallowing in self pity', to come to the forefront again. No one blamed Isobel for the accident. Not the police; not Andrew; not even the family of the unfortunate student in the car with her. Initially they had grieved together but the sorrow shared by Andrew and Isobel had gradually morphed into resentment. Andrew of Isobel for withdrawing from life; Isobel of Andrew for not.)

On his return from the races Andrew was greeted with Isobel's progress.

"It's beginning to make sense why Bernanos is in the collection. There are religious, military and political works in there too – like minds perhaps."

Isobel muttered the next words "but, hopefully, not embracing all his views" before returning proper to her subject. "I've made a list and divided them up into categories: those I've just mentioned plus poetry, music, novels, and miscellaneous."

She moved over to the sideboard, from where she picked up a few books and booklets.

"Horse racing could have been another category. But I suppose you already knew that." She handed over the volumes of *Horses in Training* together with several race cards – the details of which she had not concerned herself with.

"Oh, what's this?" Andrew asked as he took possession.

"Don't tell me you didn't know they were there." Her tone gave no indication of humour, or of anything else.

Andrew had not decided to what extent he would feign surprise at books on racing, and this discovery of previously unnoticed race cards allowed for a genuine response.

"No, I didn't know there was all this. I had seen the odd *Horses in Training* but this is great!"

The Ebor race meeting ran over four days. When Andrew came home on the second day he was struck by a change in Isobel's countenance, a quickening in the eye. But when she spoke it was with caution.

"He was called Alexander … the man from the house near Leyburn … the man with the books. He was called Alexander"

Andrew took her hands in his. He remembered and understood. Their baby was to have been Alexander if a boy, Alexandra if a girl. They hugged, briefly and awkwardly; she pulled away. Isobel talked as she mashed a pot of tea; as she paced the room; as she rummaged and messed up previously well ordered groups of books, paper, and ephemera.

"It's incredible! It really is. There are inscriptions in quite a lot of the books – and there's the odd note … and letters. I've learned **so** much about him!"

Andrew interjected with grunts and umms occasionally, until he had adjusted to the new regime, had got the gist of Isobel's project; and then sat back to let it flow.

"Alexander's the family name. The vast majority *(of books)* belonged to Albert. His widow Constance rarely features. ... In fact, I'm wondering if he didn't marry until late in life – or she was his second wife or something, because he was an adult by 1933 – Sir Charles Petrie's *Monarchy* was given to him as a belated twenty-first birthday present, with a comment about waiting to receive it from the publisher – and the first dated reference to Constance is not until the 1970s."

Her voice softened. "I've quite taken to Albert Alexander. He was obviously a caring, sensitive man. ... This is interesting, look."

Isobel passed to Andrew a programme of a choral concert (cost three pence) 'In Support of the Creswell Colliery Disaster', quickly followed by a newspaper cutting; both dated 1950. Andrew had barely time to read of the eighty dead before two further programmes, each in aid of a Society for Mentally Handicapped Children were thrust in his direction. Isobel speeded her delivery.

"Note that in the Creswell programme 'The Ash Grove' is arranged by Albert Alexander ... section two ...*(Isobel paused, Andrew duly put his finger against the entry)* and that it is sung by 'The Wilkinson Singers'. They also feature in the other two programmes."

Isobel murmured "Though they don't sing 'The Ash Grove' at those concerts", at the same time as she gathered up a stash of competition adjudication sheets and put them next to Andrew, on the sofa to which he had just moved and settled on. There was no real purpose to her putting them there, other than she had followed behind Andrew and it was convenient to let go of some of the evidence.

"Don't bother reading all those ... they're from all over – Stainforth, Stockton, Cleethorpes, Pontefract, Selston ... and of different choirs" she advised.

"It took me a while to spot the significance. Then I saw that some of the sheets were for the Wilkinson Singers – but not all – and Albert Alexander was the conductor on the remainder ..." (*More murmurings from Isobel.*) "I'd like to know if the Wilkinson Singers competed against the others at any time but there is only one adjudication per competition. ... None of the choirs sang 'The Ash Grove' – perhaps the competition rules were prescriptive about choice – but there **is** an **actual copy** of it."

Isobel held on to the music, staring at it as though she were seeing it for the first time. "It's probably in his own hand. And if it is, so is this other piece."

She held with it an untitled score, on the reverse of which were four lines by Tennyson. Isobel read out the title, 'Love Thou Thy Land'. Presumably, in the silence that followed, she was reading the whole.

"I wonder if these are words Alexander has put to this music. It would be lovely to hear it played. Who do we know who could help with that?" Isobel asked Andrew. He answered quickly. He wanted to show he was listening, and interested.

"Oh, I'm sure we could find someone. There's ..." Andrew began to list possibilities amongst their friends – but Isobel was not registering their names, she had turned to a book she had put aside. She picked it up but did not open it, nor refer to it immediately.

"Some of the competitions were for 'Mineworkers Male Voice Choirs'. Obviously he had connections to that industry. But that has no bearing on magisterial duties, does it?" Isobel went on to answer her own question. "No. I'm sure anyone can be a magistrate."

Another change of direction and her train of thought became clearer to Andrew.

"But it may give another clue as to his interest in Bernanos – he studied law. And Albert Alexander was a magistrate, served for ten years at least. – Is there a maximum you can serve? – Anyway, in the 1980s A.A. *(an abbreviation written in the book)* received 'Cromwell' by Buchan to mark the occasion, with a warm inscription, acknowledging it to be a strange gift to give a monarchist."

"Interesting." Andrew remarked. "I didn't know Bernanos knew law. I'll have to read him now we have an English translation."

"**We** have?" Isobel mocked.

For something more to say – and because of relief that Isobel had become absorbed in something outside of herself – Andrew gave some words of encouragement.

"You've done remarkably well Issy. You've created a biography from a box of books. ... What do you think others might construe from our belongings?"

They were words well meant but not thought through; did he really want Isobel to turn in on herself again? To think of how she and her life might appear to others? He regretted his words and their effect. Isobel closed down further communication until shortly before they retired for the night.

"Andrew, have you looked at the *Horses in Training* at all?" She sounded sharp and accusative of laziness.

"A little." (They were not the type of books to read cover to cover and Andrew was 'a little' irritated at the intimation he did not appreciate his booty.)

"Did you spot any clues?" Isobel asked.

"Clues to what?"

"To Albert Alexander's life, of course."

"I wasn't looking for any. Didn't even know of Albert Alexander until this evening did I? What sort of clues could there be from *Horses in Training?*"

"I don't know really. But why would he have those specific years? Are the race cards for the same period as the *Horses in Training*? I didn't notice. Did you?"

"I think they were. I'll look through them tomorrow morning." (Further irritation: with himself this time. He had just committed time he would prefer to spend going through the race card for the third day at York.)

Andrew kept to his word. It turned out to be not quite the onerous task he had envisaged. The cards covered meetings at tracks from Pontefract to Kelso and the races began two years after the first of the *Horses in Training* volumes. Andrew surmised they followed a particular horse. He worked on that assumption and concentrated on scanning the cards for a recurring name. Although he found many names repeated, there was only one to appear on every card. The horse was Quercus the Second, owned by the Wilkinson Group. Eureka!

He proudly relayed the Wilkinson connection to a grateful Isobel and turned his attention to picking out his horses for that afternoon.

The name of the horse, Quercus, caused a stirring; Isobel was inclined to go out too, though not to the races.

She followed her instinct and went to the widow's house. If she had not recalled Andrew's description of the location it would have been of no consequence; the address was on two letters secreted in the box.

There was a lopsided 'For Sale' notice by the gate ("the roots of the *Quercus* tree are affecting its stability" Isobel deduced). She had no wish to buy; no wish to look inside even; just to pass by, loiter a little. A nearby bench would have been useful, but in its absence Isobel sat in the car and ... simply looked. Looked and let her mind drift where it would. It is difficult to say whether her thoughts directed her eyes or her eyes the thoughts, but when they flitted from the oak and fixed on an ash (both in such a small front garden!), she was hit with a realization that the trees had particular meaning in Albert Alexander's life.

Not until she became conscious of someone on the opposite pavement watching her watching the house, did she begin her homeward drive.

By the time she reached home, all was clear. Albert had had a child, whom he had lost. Possibly it was a double tragedy; his first wife, the child's mother, had died at the same time. The trees commemorated their lives: the ash one life, the oak a second loss.

Isobel took from its envelope the letter addressed to 'Dear Aunt Constance'. The contents inferred a decline in her health. Nephew William had written years earlier too, to both Uncle Albert and Aunt Constance, confirming arrangements for a meeting at Pontefract. Isobel sought and found that letter. But a re-read did not clarify whether the Pontefract meet was to attend a music festival or a racetrack. A gut feeling said music, but Isobel did not go to the adjudication sheets for verification. She had become too intent on making contact with William to prevaricate.

The telephone number was a landline. So much the better as far as Isobel was concerned; she liked the level of formality and readily accepted the increased chance of having to leave a message in the first instance. This she prepared. It proved useful. A male voice picked up immediately and recited the dialled number. In spite of her thumping heart and breathlessness (which can well be imagined), Isobel did manage to read out the first planned line in front of her.

"I'm trying to contact William, the nephew of Constance Alexander."

"Speaking. ... What can I do for you?"

It was happening too quickly. There was no time to assess whether the next line fitted with William's response.

"I hope you don't mind my contacting you. I got your number from a letter you wrote to your aunt. It was in a box of Albert Alexander's books."

"Oh? ... Was it a personal letter?"

For a moment Isobel wished he had not been at home, or that she had written a letter instead of phoning.

" ... Umm ... not particularly." She rushed back to her planned speech. "The box contained Mr Alexander's musical arrangement of 'The Ash Grove' and I wondered if you would like it returned."

"Really? ... How kind of you. ... I'm not a singer myself but I have a couple of cousins who are and I'm sure they'd be thrilled to have it. Thank you."

"No problem. I'll post it to you."

"Lovely. Thank you again."

Isobel was becoming more relaxed. William sounded so kind.

"Do your cousins belong to a male voice choir, may I ask?"

"Yes. Though separate ones."

"Do you think they might make use of the arrangement?"

"Very likely. Out of curiosity, if for no other reason."

(Had a degree of irreverence crept into William's voice? Isobel sensed it had and wondered if he, or his cousins were worthy of Albert's 'Ash Grove'.)

"What about Albert Alexander's children? ... Is there someone else to whom the music may mean more, perhaps?"

"There are no children. ... Look, it's very good of you to go to this trouble and I look forward to receiving Uncle Albert's manuscript, but I'm afraid I'll have to go now. Was there anything else?"

"No. Thank you. It was nice speaking with you."

"And you. ... Oh, would you return my letter to Aunt Constance as well please, with the music?"

(Isobel decided at this point not to mention the other music, on the reverse of the poem. She would keep that.)

"Of course. ... Would it be asking too much to let me know if, in future, either of the choirs does intend to sing 'The Ash Grove', publicly? I would love to hear it."

"Will do. Bye."

Isobel was shaking when she put down the phone, but proud of her achievement. She noted that William had said there *are* no children, not that there *were* no children, and respected that he had not wanted to say more.

Andrew came home to a serene Isobel. He listened to her version of events – of that day and of Albert Alexander's days – with barely a challenge.

However, he did suggest that Quercus the Second was likely so named because there had been a previous Quercus and the precise name could not be repeated – rather than the horse being a second commemoration; he did not suggest cutting down the Alexander trees and counting the rings toward further investigation. And, not wanting to appear facetious, did not ask if there was a yew – or an eborium – in the picture (the discoveries did all coincide with the Ebor meeting after all).

Andrew did not challenge Isobel's fanciful conjectures because it was a delight to see her so transformed. He readily agreed to accompany her to a recital of 'The Ash Grove', whenever and wherever it was to take place, and in return ventured to ask her to go with him to the last day of the Ebor meeting.

"Maybe next year", she replied. "That is if I'm not working. … I've decided to go back to teaching. French literature … or, whatever I can get."

Andrew made light of the momentous decision. "That's good. I'm glad I spotted the book for you then."

" …Mm … I've done some thinking about that too. … A literal translation isn't always the best – in fact rarely so – but I have a fancy to re-read *Un Mauvais Rêve*, write my own translation – maybe stay with *A Bad Dream* – and compare it with Strachan's *Night is Darkest*."

"Ambitious. And impressive. Go for it."

"And there will be no sale of books from the box", she told him. "To split up the collection would be like taking apart a life. Besides, the inscriptions would lower the value of individual books, whereas in context …"

"Quite right." Andrew agreed. … "I've had a win. Shall we eat out tonight?"

You and Me Both

◇◇◇

Meredith and Gloria had shared a secret on their first day at primary school; they had swapped drawings. Meredith had written her name at the top of Gloria's picture of a house; Gloria had written her name at the top of Meredith's picture of a family.

They are much older now.

"Can't we make it the service station at junction 24 instead?" Gloria asks Meredith – by email. (Straightforward emailing from her home computer is the limit of Meredith's concession to technology. Gloria accommodates this.)

Meredith does not oblige the request. "Sorry Gloria, but I don't understand your objection to the shopping centre; there's a seat directly opposite *Dolly's Dresses*; it's undercover, so a great place to wait in case either of us is delayed."

It is not like Meredith to be insistent. Gloria takes some time before responding. (During the past week Gloria has acquired rather a new habit, one of mulling things over rather than following her instincts at crashing speeds.)

"I know what it will be", Gloria thinks. "It's her twenty-fifth wedding anniversary coming up. She'll want to chat about outfits for the 'do'. Though can't think why she still wants my input, her husband's a damned buyer after all. And I doubt Meredith would ever be seen dead in anything from my wardrobe."

Gloria switches to imagining the contents of said wardrobe, and sinks lower into her chair as she visualizes, and realizes. "I'll have to get something new for the shindig, something that at least fits! I'll call in at the Designer Outlet en route to 24."

Gloria gently raises herself and writes "Sorry Meredith". Her fingers hover. She notes that Meredith began similarly; it might be interpreted as mocking. 'Delete'. Replaces with "Sounds like a great idea, but for next time. It's just that I've been on the road a heck of a lot and to tell you the truth I'm exhausted. Junction 24 is mid-way." 'Send'.

It's true that she feels exhausted; true that she normally travels a lot – selling is more difficult than buying, and when the 'product' is communication services, speciality interpersonal skills … well, it goes without saying that you have to prove yourself 'in person'. She has not been on the road, or been anywhere, for a few weeks. But she hasn't actually said that she has.

"Typical!" Meredith shouts at her computer. "Gloria's time is so precious she won't travel a few more meagre miles to see me."

Meredith is saddened out of all proportion. She sobs out a plea not to be rejected. "Not you too Gloria!"

Gloria, the one person Meredith counts on for reassurance.

Both of Meredith's children – children no more – plan to come back for the anniversary. But will they now? And even if they do fly over, what can she expect from them? They are his children too.

No, the immediate help has to come from Gloria; Gloria will take one look at the husband-snatching bitch and laugh at the notion she can hang on to him. She will tell Meredith, "He'll be back". Gloria knows about that business stuff. She will understand about the flirting needed to clinch a deal. 'Dolly' probably insisted on trying on dresses before she agreed to stock them; probably deliberately left a gap in the curtain to tempt him. He probably kept the affair going just to keep her on side for contracts. Contracts he could not afford to lose. They needed the money for … well everything. Meredith was not an earner. Had never been an earner.

She re-reads Gloria's response: "next time" they could meet outside the shop. That might be better: delay the telling. Meredith dreads saying the words. Dreads admitting that the marriage has failed. Nothing left. No life. What will Gloria make of that? Gloria has never married. Plenty of relationships – well that is her forte, her job isn't it – but she has never depended on anyone.

On reflection, the meeting place has to be Meredith's choice. She will assert the place – if not the time; show some strength. And when Gloria tells her how insipid 'Dolly' looks, Meredith will snigger and agree.

She writes, between the continuing sobs. "Best leave things until you feel less exhausted. Let me know when."

Gloria is asleep when Meredith's message comes in. The alarm is set for one hour before her appointment. She is lucky in that the surgery is close by. A quick wash and change of clothes and she will be on her way. She spots the new email. Some relief at a postponement is mingled with disappointment; she is desperate to see Meredith.

"Aarrgh!" Gloria screams. The pain takes her by surprise.

She uses a hand against the chair arm for balance. The next pain comes sharper still. She makes a dash forward, but doesn't make it out of the room. "What on earth was I thinking of? I can't make it from bedroom to bathroom, let alone make the motorway with some godforsaken detour to buy a frock!"

Gloria resolves, she will hear the doctor out this time and take any palliative care offered – if that will give her energy enough to do the necessary: to see Meredith; share a few favourite memories; and ask Meredith to help sort out the domestic arrangements. A useful phrase Gloria thinks. She has frequently used it to cover all aspects of work venues. Now, she can apply it to requirements whilst she remains in her flat, and wherever her 'venue' thereafter. She has no family or significant other in her life. Her one and only true friend, Meredith, will be perfectly capable of dealing with these matters, the sorts of things families do.

Timing is the thing. Gloria does not want to come across as some pathetic weakling. Goodness knows she has little enough to show for her efforts. She will keep her doctor's appointment – wearing a pad and three pairs of knickers if she has to – and, in the light of what the doctor says, make a judgement. When and where she can make it to see Meredith.

Out of Sync

◇◇◇

"Sorry", he said at every perceived misdemeanour: a word spoken too readily, irritatingly so.

"Sorry" – when he interrupted, unintentionally before she had finished speaking. "Sorry" to have taken so long to make her a cup of coffee – kettle filled beyond minimum needed. "Sorry" to have switched to another television channel – she was still reading the credits.

"Stop apologizing" she would say. But it was not kindly meant. She thought him pathetic. This change in him was pathetic. She had not minded when he told her to stop nattering on, or to get on with the meal woman. To her it was just part of their banter. As she reminded her friends, if he had been a male chauvinist he was unlikely to have taken her country dancing every fortnight. It was never his choice – "not strictly dancing, more prancing". He had gone only to please her.

But he was not pleasing her now. They never went country dancing; no longer dined out; no longer had days away, let alone a proper holiday.

It seemed like a hundred times a day she would hear the hiss of a sorry coming: one hundred and one and she would have to scream and leave! Why couldn't it be 'Sorry I've not taken you out' instead of hissing over nothing!

At first, she too had been devastated. Not for herself, you understand, but for him. Redundancies had been spoken of but he had not thought it could apply to him. When it did, it came as a shock. She appreciated that.

However, she adjusted her thinking quite quickly. She could see the positives. They were not badly off for money; more leisure time together would be like an extended weekend. And there were shopping trips with friends whilst he played golf – or whatever – to look forward to.

None of that happened. He became mean; said they needed to re-plan for their retirement before they started spending; so self-pitying.

He had been a good sales and marketing manager, no one said otherwise. *Display Designs* had continued to grow throughout his twenty-three years with them. There had been a change of focus that was all.

The first contracts (with just four shops) had been to provide the designs for window displays. All required props and the personnel (a recent graduate from an art and design college) to do the actual dressing. The more lucrative contracts were with fashion establishments – regular changes almost guaranteed to increase footfall across the threshold. And where space permitted, further tableaux inside the shops encouraged the customer to linger that bit longer, increase the chances of a purchase. In fact 'linger-longer' was a term adopted for such an addition: "How about a linger-longer, placed here, to highlight your new dinner-at-home evening wear?"

He was proud of how he rarely failed to renew a contract (other than on occasion when a shop changed hands); and, for the first seven years, year on year he doubled the number of their clients. Of course, once into the hundreds it became more difficult to expand so exponentially, even with the help of assistants.

The company took another leap forward when they transferred some of their efforts to the Internet. One, then suddenly a dozen graduates (a bit risky but undeniably it had worked) – from combinations of IT, graphic design and arty-type backgrounds – took things in hand. Amazing really. There was the simple advertizing of the company: examples of their stunning window displays synergistically promoted the designer and the merchandiser – for which many a seller was willing to pay handsomely. Expertly done. But, more significantly for the sales and marketing departments, subsequent negotiations could also be done without the need for expensive travel costs and man-hours.

The virtual design team (a misnomer perhaps; the team did actually exist but designed on-screen) arranged everything for their 'partners' (as new 'clients' were known) from design to delivery of props and, as before, expert personnel to service the contract, without leaving a screen. The window dressers did turn up, physically, to bring the agreed design to life – as if by magic – from a few clicks on a keyboard.

It was not as though, at 58 years old, he was reluctant to change. It was merely that others had beaten him to it. He had been slow to realize he was in a race until they had passed the winning post.

His booby prize was early retirement. Investments, income (where was it going to come from?) and outgoings all had to be viewed with a different eye. He could not rush the process and she would have to be patient, allow him time and space to think.

After five months of thinking, assessing and planning – but before he was quite ready to launch into discussion with his wife – a letter came from *Display Designs*.

The gist of the letter was that, should he be interested, they were able to offer him a new post. Sadly, there was no opening of a similar standing to that which he had occupied previously, but it was hoped this one would have some appeal. There was no question of his ability to carry out the duties and so, should he be willing to return to *Display Designs,* he need only to let them know of his acceptance. His expertize would always be an asset.

He read the letter in silence, then passed it to his wife while he skim read the accompanying pages of blurb.

She was ecstatic! He was unmoved.

How brilliant! She could not find words enough to express her exhilaration (few were needed, her joy was obvious). It was such a relief to be able to go back to how they had been.

"We will have to see" was his non-committal response.

"But Georgie …"

He had long since outgrown 'Georgie', whatever the tone employed. In their early days such a preface to any request would ensure she got her way. Not now. George interrupted her protestation and handed her the other documents as he headed towards the kitchen, saying "We won't be lunching out today Rachel (*he made a point of not using his pet name for her*) but I'll do you a bacon and tom if you like."

Lunching out was one of the luxuries, enjoyed particularly by Rachel, which had fallen by the wayside. To draw attention to the fact struck Rachel as rather cruel, but she was not prepared to spite her stomach in protest: she nodded her acceptance, smiled her thanks, and turned her attention to the job description and terms and conditions that had been handed to her.

The post offered looked attractive enough at first glance. He would be the face of *Display Designs*. Once the virtual team had completed all that was needed to secure and fulfil the contracts, George would visit the establishments, view the displays and ensure client satisfaction. His visits would be strategically timed to closely precede the end date of a current contract. (Similarities to work he had done previously were somewhat disguised in the wording, but clear enough to George.) It was an important post, obviously, as renewal of contracts (client satisfaction) was crucial to the company's long-term success. But, obviously, not as important as had been the work he had done previously. One third of the importance, judging by the salary offered.

Discussion of what was to be the next step taken was left until after the bacon and tomato sandwiches had been eaten. Both tacitly agreed that a bacon sandwich was one enjoyment that should not be compromised.

Rachel, not seeing any real obstacle to regaining her pleasant lifestyle, began the conversation with an assumption that George would return to the full time employment offered. The last five months had been miserable. She had become quite anxious about the future. He must have noticed – despite all attempts to hide her disappointments – how down her mood had become. And now, their worries were over. When would he start back? When would be a reasonable time to take a holiday? Didn't he long to go walking in the Peak District again?

George answered only the first of the questions posed. He would not be returning to work at *Display Designs*. Had she not taken note of the salary?

It was less. Yes, it was a great deal less than he had earned previously. But wouldn't the new job be less stressful? And it wasn't as though they needed a large income now that the mortgage had been repaid. There was no need to add to their savings but his having an income, at all, would allow for them to enjoy life without being concerned about depleting the amount they had put by for retirement proper.

Rachel was pleased with her reasoned, if impromptu, argument. George appeared to have been stunned into silence. Then he re-iterated "I will not be going back".

He was reluctant to explain fully his reasons, believing she would not understand. But "Why?" "Why?" forced an attempt.

George said he did not want to sound over dramatic or "corny" but the redundancy had forced him to re-evaluate his life. One thing they could agree on, it was an opportunity for something positive to happen. Perhaps where they differed was on what that something should be.

For five months he had been scrutinizing their spending patterns; separating essential from non-essential elements and of the non-essential, which were truly desirable and which were merely habit – no doubt this would be another area of disagreement. On the income side, he had calculated how long the redundancy package, alongside his private pension – the timing of the claim was still in abeyance – would support spending on essentials and desirables. He had been pleasantly surprised at his findings.

George's conclusion was that his most desirable non-essential – to go rock climbing – would be affordable.

Rachel was horrified and "Sorry George, I think you're having a mid-life crisis" was her conclusion.

She argued that wanting a new interest was no reason to reject an income for a while longer. So far, he had gone no way to explain why he would not take the job.

He turned the question around; but before he asked why he should go back to work he expanded on why the offer had served to strengthen his determination to spend time rock climbing. It was – as she knew – not a sudden whim. He wasn't subject to whims. As a young man he had ventured into the sport and made good progress, considering the brief time he spent at it. Work and family commitments had then taken precedence.

At fifty-eight years old it was now or never to give it another go. He was not expecting miracles, he knew he would have limitations but they would only increase the longer he waited. Time had become more precious, yet the new job valued his time less.

Rachel was sorry that he seemed to regret having put her before rocks in their marriage, and asked where this now left her – besides in second place to a pile of earth's rubble! "Wherever you want to be" was the answer given.

There would be money enough for some dining out and country dancing – though she may need to find another dancing/prancing partner. Reckless shopping sprees – with or without her friends – were not within the new budget. That said, if shopping malls were where she most wanted to be then she might want to consider going back to work. A managerial post in a shop would be ideal; she had plenty of experience. If none was available, perhaps she would accept something that paid less, but would at least be an income. Her choice. He had made his.

Rachel was sorry that she could not bring herself to agree with George's decision or persuade him to change his mind.

Today is History

◇◇◇

Seeds sown. All grown. Such is life and no more.

Mum bakes. She takes. In silence, from the resented mother-in-law who saw that look, that gesture, that tells what's gone before.

It's piercing, the silence.

Those from other mothers, they don't want to hear what dear old ladies have to say. Old mums and grans have had their day.

To break the piercing silence, Mum chatters, natters. Bores. Knows. She saw that look, that gesture, that tells what's gone before.

It's sore, the knowing.

Mum goes to bed, because it's time to go away, because, today, life is too much.

New Riches

◇◇◇

Mrs Pincher, widowed, goes out every day. She can well afford to now. In her words "Could not afford not to". And anyway it's "Good for the soul" she says.

She was devastated when her husband died, not that I knew her then. It was a great emotional loss, of course, but also a financial one. Both retired at the same time, aged 60, early for those times. His was a much bigger work's pension than hers and, as interest rates were sky high they plumped for a maximum bird in the hand strategy; invested the spare and built up their own fund.

Worked well, she says. No regrets. But, they were in their ninth decade when he died. High interest rates had long been a thing of the past and the fund had dwindled, considerably. Much less left for that rainy day.

Not surprisingly, his death left her terrified. How on earth was she going to manage on her meagre pension?

By the time I met Mrs Pincher those worries were over. She shops at the same supermarket as I do and we bump into each other frequently – not literally you understand; we both like to take advantage of the in-store café, have a sit down and partake of the complimentary, loyalty cup of tea. Or coffee if preferred. (Mrs Pincher always has coffee. For her, tea has to be so weak it's hardly worthy of the name, and no self-respecting dispenser of it will serve it to suit. So, coffee it is.) I usually buy a meal to have with the drink, and a cake or something, but she brings her own. Though, now that we've taken to sitting together she will occasionally share a little of my dessert. A lady of simple food tastes. Unadventurous? Certainly not; not in other ways anyhow.

The way Mrs Pincher has come through her bereavement is an inspiration to us all. She says the pain and the sudden panics become like snow blizzards in April: unexpected, sharp and severe, but pass more quickly. She's right on the money with that one.

I so love to chat with her. On those days when she doesn't come into the supermarket it amuses me to think where she might be. Has she gone to the coast for the day? Or taken two or three connecting buses to a new big city? … Can you believe this? – Mrs Pincher knows the timetables and bus routes of nearly all the services off by heart. Not only from her local bus station: the bus pass takes you nationwide. Amazing! And her house is so close to the main bus station she can get there on foot.

That was her first stroke of luck. And no need to move when her husband died because, as a lone occupant, the council taxes dropped. She hadn't realized that would happen. But on reflection it makes sense. She doesn't use their services to the same extent now does she; less rubbish to dispose of, and so on. The water rates have come down drastically too. Though they aren't part of the council services as she had once thought. Apparently, it had been a really good idea of her husband's to switch to a meter for the water. He had them occasionally: good ideas that is. Though, by all accounts thinking wasn't his main activity.

Mrs Pincher is very active for her age. Well, I suppose sitting on buses doesn't use up much energy but she does still garden. Not to the same extent as her husband did – nothing seems to be to the same extent: it's a phrase she uses a lot – but she spent time after he died mooching around outside, and has got into a new habit.

It is quite a revelation how many dishes can be made, or supplemented, with the likes of broad beans, or leeks. She has always been a reasonable cook, she tells me, but by foraging (over two seasons – she had had no idea of the variety and magnitude of his planting; new things emerged one after another. Surely, there must have been a lot gone to waste in the past she thinks) and using her initiative, she produces plates that any Master Chef would be proud to place before Greg and Jon. (Must make a note to raise the possibility of her actually entering for *Masterchef* when we next chat.)

Some of the produce can be kept going … potatoes and so on. If a seed can be collected, or a few potatoes or beans (I suppose they are seeds too, of a sort) saved, they can all be replanted. At no cost whatsoever! Now that she finds doubly rewarding, to harvest and eat what she has grown herself. (Keeping chickens had crossed her mind. There would be extra protein from the eggs and the occasional old bird to eat. But coming across a fertilized egg – let alone then raising the chicken – has, so far, proved a tad too difficult, even for Mrs Pincher.)

On her away days she packs up her food in the same manner as when we dine together – enough for two meals if it is going to be a long journey. (At present she has entitlement to only one free cup of tea or coffee a day. But her loyalty may be divided between two supermarkets in the future and she may get a second one by virtue of that. Both are big names and a store can be found in any town she visits.)

Another point of luck, for Mrs Pincher, is to have been "blessed with a good bladder". Distance is not a limiting factor. There is always a lavatory to be found at the stations, or nearby, and she always allows time to make use of the facility, which includes the one at her local bus station: if the day is well planned, and she has not over-indulged on the hot tea-water at breakfast, she can hold on until after she has left the house – she tells me I would be surprised how much water one flush uses!

Mrs Pincher is not a martyr to her outings. That is to say, she does not venture out in icy weather, or if snow risks the cancellation of buses. She stays home and puts on the heating. There is no danger of her not being able to pay the heating bills. No Siree. Not now. Mrs Pincher will never take to wearing her wardrobe and burning the shell to keep warm. Not her style, she says. She saves enough on fine days to cover bleak ones.

Today is a day spent close to home and I see her approaching the café. She looks a million dollars. Dressed in a young two-tone fashion; a broad band of green around the hemline, neckline and sleeves, the body a bright floral print. I greet her with "Penny, you look incredible. Is that a new dress?"

"Bless you, no. I've taken apart a couple of tired old ones and given them a new lease of life."

A Tale out of School

◇◇◇

Mr Brookes patted my golden bonnet, closed out the light, locked the garage door and set off for the bus to take him to the railway station. How long was it going to be before I next saw the light of day, let alone have a run out?

It was not as though I were a youngster: quite old enough to be left on my own in the station car park, in my opinion. But then no one would be asking for my views any time soon. My previous owners never listened; their little brat had kicked the life out of the back of my driver's seat, but did they care? No. Finally I just had to let rip.

A good move, as it turned out. When Mr Brookes took proud possession, he kindly arranged to have me brought back to my former glory: a painful process but I'm comfortable now. And I'm so grateful he let me keep my red leather interior. I have no false modesty; I know there is no better Humber Sceptre to be found. I should be allowed out more, that's my only complaint.

The garage light comes on, from the kitchen access. Whenever James – a friend of Mrs Brookes' – visits me he always comes through the house, never the garden.

James sits on my passenger seat and takes a few exercise books from his briefcase. He switches on my interior light. This is much better; the title on the opened page of the top book on the small pile is clearly visible. *There are mixed messages in Anna Karenina. Discuss.* But I have no chance to read the discussion; James's phone rings and, for some less than obvious reason, he turns off my light.

I am not too disappointed; *Anna Karenina* is beyond my comprehension. *A day in the life of a stamp* was simpler but had held no interest. I live in hope of *A day in the life of a car*. Now that would be something to read of; I never get to meet any other cars these days and it does get kind of lonely.

James speaks softly to his caller. He laughs as he says "Well, you're sixteen now. I'm sure something can be arranged."

Mrs Brookes unwittingly disrupts the call. "James, are you there?" She spots him and, somewhat unnecessarily announces, "Ah, yes, you are." She asks him what he is doing.

James says "Just finishing off a bit of marking: all done now. You going to join me?"

She says not. Absolutely firm about it. She leaves. James moves over to my driving seat. (The usual practice, which I do not much like, is for Mrs Brookes and James to rock me about a bit from the rear seat; the rocking is not so bad but they are none too careful with my interior and I do not want another bruising or tear.)

James turns over my engine. This brings Mrs Brookes straight back and onto the seat he has recently warmed (my leather can be a little cold in winter, I can't help that).

"I'd love to take this baby for a spin. ... Half-term next week ... What do you say Mrs B?"

Mrs Brookes says it would be more than her life is worth.

"He'll never know. Not if we get off nice 'n early." James clicks a few buttons and pulls on a lever that sets off my wipers. He's a bit rough compared to Mr Brookes. "And we'll get back before him – but after it's dark. The neighbours won't see us if we don't turn towards Main Street. What's the harm?"

James gives her a moment to digest the notion. Well, barely a moment really, before he comes back with "It's safer than me hanging around the house. We can have more time together", he coaxes. And looks away from my dashboard, into her eyes. "I hate just popping in and rushing off again."

Mrs Brookes says she hates that too. Sighs. Agrees to the jaunt.

I want to cheer right along there with James! Daylight; fresh air; a day motoring. What joy!

◇◇◇

James and Mrs B are as good as their words. Mr Brookes leaves for work and here they are, both excited to be taking me out.

James looks different in his dark grey balaclava; and Mrs Brookes, rather puzzlingly, chooses to squat in front of my glove compartment for the first part of the journey.

We go out into the country and I am able to show off a little; demonstrate the comfort I afford at really quite impressively high speeds. And ... Oh, what a sight! It is years since I last saw the sea. It is such a pleasure that I do not object in the least when James and Mrs Brookes take to the back seat for a few minutes. The wind is buffeting my outer body and I hardly notice the counter movement inside.

Neither do I mind when they leave me on my own for a while, even though I have no company from other cars. It is so good to be out.

All too soon, James and Mrs Brookes come back. It is much, much too soon. I am not ready to go back to the garage. So, when James tries to start my engine, I refuse to co-operate.

He tries and tries. He makes a study of a few of my mechanical bits, and then tries again. But I am determined; I am not going anywhere.

James and Mrs Brookes argue. Mrs Brookes shouts, "This is it. The End. If I'm not there when he gets back – and the car gone! – I'm finished. I can't drive. I can't pretend I've taken it out. What can we do?"

"For God's sake calm down. There's no problem if you stay calm" James says.

Mrs Brookes does calm down. She thinks, calmly. And comes up with a plan.

"We'll come clean. About us, I mean. Then we don't have to invent a story of what's happened to the car. He'll be more bothered about getting the damned car back than me. So, it will make it all easier." Mrs Brookes warms to the idea as she speaks. The remedy gathers momentum. "In fact, it's good timing. If you're honest about seeing me, you'll also be able to clear your name of those filthy slurs. Prove that the accusations are false; tell them, at last, that you were with me every time and not with any deluded, besotted adolescent."

I can feel the shock go through James. It is not a solution that has occurred to him. Mrs Brookes begins to elucidate some more "I will tell …"

"Don't you dare mention me to anyone" James warns, not at all calmly. He seems to have forgotten his own advice. He rushes his next, sharply spoken words. "You know I can't leave yet, not with Barbara how she is. I can't do such a thing to my poorly daughter, you have to accept that."

He does not give Mrs B an opportunity to challenge the precept but does deliver the next directive a little more slowly – and loudly. "And keep out of school stuff. Right out! I only mentioned it in case you heard rumours." He gets out and shouts over his shoulder as he leaves me. "What we've to do is just get you back home before him. We'll think on the way. Just move it …"

Mrs Brookes grabs her bag and runs to catch up.

◇◇◇

Dark has descended when a re-balaclava-ed James returns, fuel can in hand. Surely he doesn't think an empty tank was the reason I wouldn't start! Does he understand nothing? I thought he cared. I thought he brought me out for a run because he appreciated how desperate I was to be out of the garage.

James walks around me. What is this that is happening? I feel a wet splashing around my tyres; around my bumpers. Fumes seep inside. James stands still. He peers through my windscreen.

Good. I want to be admired. I muster every scrap of energy, take extra from the moonlight; rays flow over my blood red interior; my bonnet flashes its gold.

Sirens sound and interrupt my preening.

I hear James sob. He throws one lighted match at me, then another. I hear the rustle of his coat as he flees. I hear a low rumbling and a crackling as my body warms. I hear voices from behind the bright flash of torches. They yell, "Stop. Police". The engulfing heat is unbearable. I strain to hear anything else. But I think I hear "A write-off".

At the Centre

◇◇◇

Doreen knew the nuances of machines and bus passes; she snatched up her pass on the ding of authorization and mounted the stairs with determined sprite. One of the front window seats was vacant – not a surprise to Doreen, she had checked out that possibility on the bus's approach.

The lady on the adjacent seat must have been only half the age of Doreen; an assessment made as quickly as the time it took Doreen to observe the driver's hesitancy to pull away. "I don't know why he's so long in setting off, there wasn't exactly a queue of people to get on!" Doreen directed this comment towards the younger lady.

The explanation – "Oh, he's a good man this one. He's waited for you to be settled" – was quite expected, and the perfect opportunity to reassure the stranger, in no uncertain terms, that it had been unnecessary to wait. "In fact I'm fitter than most people half my age". (Doreen gave the lady another sideways glance). No offence was taken at the inference, or if it was it was not apparent in the response. "I can well believe it. Fitter than me at any rate."

Doreen had made her point, clearly and as intended. But she was not proud of herself ... She reflected. Had she, perhaps, been insensitive? Was the stranger ill? She could have cancer or something; lots of medical problems aren't obvious.

Take John. He seemed totally well up to two months before he died. Funny two months they had been. Unreal. It seems an age ago, and as yesterday all at the same time. The day of the diagnosis – their daughter Barbara's birthday – is the first imprint; then up to his death – on her own birthday – is what defines the two months, otherwise without measure: oblivious of hours, days, weeks, months. A lifetime's joys or a lifetime's pains condensed in an unexpected moment, over and over.

Search for the joy, she thought. Search for the joy. And ventured to say

"It's so worth sitting here, isn't it? You can see for miles on the stretch between South Milford and Garforth. And even weaving through that massive housing estate is less tedious. You can have a neb at the gardens. (*The stranger half smiled, Doreen rattled on.*) Do you do this journey much? Have you ever noticed that enormous bear carved out of a tree trunk? Amazing! In such a tiny garden too. And the next door's garden is so big, with nothing in it. ... Oh, it's just occurred to me. Do you suppose that's why they've got the bear – to emphasize the difference? ... Empty vastness compared to small but interesting?"

The stranger frowned: in thought or anger? Doreen wondered again; had she been insensitive? Did this woman live on the estate, in the bear garden, or the bare garden even? Doreen thought it best to move the conversation on.

"My name's Doreen by the way. I'm going into Leeds then out to the garden centre."

"Nice to meet you *Daw*-reen. I'm Jane."

"Actually, everyone calls me Dorrie." (It was a preferred option to *Daw*-reen, but Doreen didn't add her reasoning.)

Staying on safe ground for a while, Dorrie spoke of her own garden – of the wide borders, a cottage style; the seats strategically placed to capture sun when sought, shade when needed.

"It sounds lovely" Jane acknowledged, and asked Dorrie what she hoped to find at the garden centre. Was it anything special or was she just going to browse?

Dorrie was quiet for a moment, as though considering her answer. Instead she posed a question of her own.

"Are you interested in gardening Jane?"

Jane wasn't, not especially. That is, not in doing any actual work. But she could, and did appreciate the efforts of others and enjoyed visiting gardens.

"So you don't have your own garden?" Dorrie asked.

"Just a few yards that mark the territory around the house: mainly grassed with the odd shrub."

And so they continued, each coming to describe a little more detail of their plantings.

It was during one of Dorrie's contributions that the bus approached a busy junction. Dorrie stopped mid-sentence. And remained silent, until Jane's prompt.

"You were saying, ... the rose bush ..."

The bus crossed into a free lane. "Oh yes. Sorry. It was force of habit. I always stopped talking to let John concentrate on driving when we met other traffic. ... Do you know, I don't think John liked houseplants? ... Or maybe we didn't have any because of my attitude towards them *(Dorrie grimaced at the thought)*. I don't believe I actually said. But, for once, he might have picked up on what I was thinking."

Jane, in turn, picked up on the theme. "I take it a search for house geraniums are not on the agenda today then." She spoke with a gentle good humour, in contrast to Dorrie's abrasive tone.

"Oh, I'm pretty sure it's on my daughter's agenda – it's her idea to meet at the garden centre. Her agenda for how I should organize my life now; how I should make everything 'manageable' for a solitary old woman.

"What do you make of this notion of 'bringing the outside in and taking the inside out' Jane? *(A rhetorical question apparently.)* I think it's a nonsense! The idea of having a house and a garden is to get relief and pleasure from each as mood and opportunity dictate.

"When you've done the necessary in the house you don't want to have to start tendering pot plants as well, do you? You just want to sit down, have a cup of tea and watch a bit of TV or read a book. And when you're fed up with the sight of four walls, you want to potter outside in the garden; look at how the plants are doing, at what new things have blown in – and sit on your weathered wooden seat in the midst of it all. Not start wiping down and dusting furniture and clutter in some new-fangled summer house!

"Same applies to 'dining out' type meals for at home, and going out to where they serve 'good home cooking'. Either go out or stay in. What's wrong with keeping the two experiences separate!

"Barbara says they *(she gives a nod to the visualized garden centre)* do a cottage pie that tastes just like mine. … I rest my case."

Jane chuckled and gave Dorrie a warm smile, the like of which Dorrie had not seen in quite a while.

A tear dropped from Dorrie's eye as she tried to transpose that same smile and pleasure she saw in Jane's eyes onto the face of Barbara; to replace Barbara's permanent mix of concern and irritation, never joy.

"Why don't you postpone your trip to the garden centre" Jane suggested, "and join me at Le Nez. Now. In the city centre – for some fine dining?"

Dorrie caught her breath. With surprise, relief, excitement? Whatever the reason, she took out her phone to contact Barbara, immediately. This turn of events might do them both good.

She and Jane exchanged girlish grins. Dorrie felt twenty years younger. When the bus arrived at the station she went down the stairs ahead of Jane, light of foot, and dignified.

Independence Day

◇◇◇

"No need for a wash this morning – I'm still clean from yesterday's swill" … She sniffs at a pile of clothes. Picks out a pair of knickers … "and these are fresh enough; it's been a good week on that front."

Dorrie is not demented; no, she speaks her thoughts so as to keep her voice strong and familiar.

"I've got over an hour to get myself to the kitchen. … She'll ring at eleven. …Why fix the phone *there* of all places? *So* inconvenient! … She'll offer to take me to the hospital today. I'll let her. If I don't turn up this time, that will be it: dishonourable discharge!"

Ten o'clock, the phone rings.

"She's early. She must have 'other plans'. Wants to get me over and done with does she. Well, I'm not her charity case."

Dorrie pulls herself up on her frame and makes her way to the kitchen.

"Hello Mum, it's Babs."

"Barbara, you don't have to announce who you are: who else would it be?"

"How are you Mother? How's that foot?"

"A damn sight worse for having to traipse to the kitchen to answer the phone."

"That's why I got you the mobile, Mum. Why don't you use it?"

"You know why not! I tried it and it doesn't work."

"Mum. That was only the once; when I was in Cumbria and couldn't get a signal. If you would just keep it switched on and with you, I'd be able to phone you without causing you this bother every time."

"Well I can't hold the phone and this damn frame at the same time, now can I? So, I can't very well have it 'with' me, as you say."

"Once your foot is better you won't need the frame ... and that's partly why I'm ringing. Isn't it your appointment today? I was planning to come down to Sally's, so, I could easily pick you up and take you to the hospital on the way."

"No, thank you. No need to put yourself out."

"It wouldn't be putting me out at all. I want to see you. And I might as well make myself useful. What time is your appointment? This afternoon, is it? I could come early and do a bit round the house for you first, if you like ... or we could just have a catch-up chat?"

"Just a moment please Barbara."

Dorrie lets go of the receiver and flexes her fingers.

"Useless digits!"

She sniffs. "What's that rank smell? ... Ugh! It'll be the smoked mackerel wrapping; that bin needs emptying."

She looks around the kitchen and assesses its state, through Barbara's eyes.

"A mess. She'll say, again, that it's time to get me help. The first step ..."

Dorrie re-grips the receiver.

"Actually Barbara I'm going out today ... to the Luncheon Club. I'm finished with the hospital. The foot is healing, slowly but surely, and they can't do anything to speed up the process."

"What about afterwards then? What time will you be back from the Luncheon Club?"

Dorrie quickly tries to calculate – How long to make the place look decent? ... More than one day's strength is needed.

"Sorry Barbara. No can do today; I'll be back late and ready for my bed. But do phone again when you have time. It's lovely to hear from you."

"Mum ... Mum ...

Dorrie puts the phone back on its hook. Looks at the clock and sighs.

"Five minutes past ten. Is that all? She could have talked for a bit longer!"

Untitled

◇◇◇

Sadly I'm not a poet, and neither is Anthony Cunningham – a character in the novel *Corkscrewed*.

But, when Mr. Cunningham recognizes how he has allowed a manipulative, abusive woman to successfully and irreversibly remove him from all his other relationships, he puts pen to paper:

> *Once in life I was and had a father, brother, son.*
> *Now I do as you bid do, and they are all but gone.*
> *Domination: Abomination in all eyes but thine.*
> *Now I'm no one, I have no one if I don't call you mine.*
> *Abomination domination. I want to return*
> *to home; to son; to a warm face in mornings he has kissed.*
> *You call and call, and shout and shout, words that I daren't resist*
>
> *for fear of being left alone in my own hell, to burn.*

He didn't give a thought to the fashion of avoiding rhyme or to any of the rules that might define good poetry. Perhaps it was because all rhyme and reason had gone from his life that he was drawn to create, even to force it. He didn't think about rhythm or meter because he expected it would never be read (it was hidden in a copy of *A Day in the Life of Ivan Denisovich* by Solzhenitsyn). He didn't consider whether to write in couplets, quatrains or an octave.

I suspect that 'real' poets do not need to consciously think of those things either. So, when is a poem a 'good' poem? What makes it 'work'; have real meaning?

Using Anthony Cunningham's poem as an example, I would suggest that – unlike his effort – a good poem does not have to be put into context, explained. It will *be* the context, *a* context, even if the context differs in the mind of each reader.

The synergy of lyrical poetry and music is well established. They share some common terms, octave and rhythm the more obvious ones. Music composition, like poetry, follows rules – the use of accidentals gives the necessary freedom to break them.

Did poets and musicians study and analyze the best pieces and thus identify the patterns that have become the rules by which to write/compose? Or were rules defined at the offset? No doubt students of poetry or music know the answer and will enlighten me in due course.

Rufus, another character in the aforementioned novel, is a songwriter. I am not. Unlike non-poet Anthony, the credibility of the character Rufus could be brought into question by my failings. Fortunately, I was given permission to take lyrics from songwriter, Steve Gardner, and use them to suit. It was a generous gesture for which I remain grateful.

Arguably, most of us are neither poets nor composers yet we follow, to some degree, the rules of syntax, punctuation, etc. Important for clarity of meaning. But who should be judge of the written word how closely one thought/sentence relates to another? The writer, the reader, the professor? Discussions of this sort are never-ending! How shall I finish? With a full stop.

Note: The lyrics I borrowed on behalf of Rufus have since featured on the album *Bathed in Comfort*, by Steve Gardner, Chuck Prophet and the Mission Express. It is interesting and delightful, to hear them in that context. Rufus would be proud.

Billingsley Roses

◇◇◇

Based on a True Story

Lavinia Billingsley is at the packed auction house. She senses the presence of her sister Sarah, and of her mother and father; though somehow they have become separated.

The auctioneer announces Lot 76:

"A modern, creamware service in the 'Billingsley Rose' pattern. Where will you start me? 100 pounds? Well, 50 then. Surely: in production during the 1970s and 1980s only. Now becoming very collectable. 50? Thank you sir … "

Lavinia is shocked. Her head screams at this irony of ironies; a rose printed on ivory earthenware. Her father's overriding goal was always to produce the whitest, most translucent porcelain known. And they copy his style of painting onto *ivory earthenware*!

" … 80, 90, 100 … 120? Are you bidding madam? No? I'll take 105. Where? This is for nothing, there's a shelf full. No more? Selling then at 100. It's still cheap."

He bangs down the hammer and moves on to Lot 77.

"A Nant-Garw porcelain plate, dating to around 1818. This is from the same estate as the previous lot: a must for any collector with an interest in William Billingsley. Several bids left on this. I can start at 900 pounds ..."

◇◇◇

William Billingsley's passion to develop his own porcelain repeatedly leads his family into debt, and incurs losses for all those willing to support him financially. His wife is not reconciled to the indulgence of this passion. It is a constant cause of friction and disagreement between them.

Mrs Sarah Billingsley: How much longer must we rely on the favours of others William? Mr Wells allows the roof over our heads; James Walker provides the labours of Samuel, and monies for the kiln, but who is to give us the bread for our mouths? Bread flour could not be bought for less than 3s 3d a stone in Brampton today.

William: Oh, stop fretting Sarah. The work will soon be completed on Samuel's new kiln. And when we are producing more of our own porcelain, what concern then the price of flour? Mm?

Mrs Billingsley: Soon you say. But how soon? All I hear is soon! Wood stocks for the parlour fire are getting low again; I hear there is to be a sale of tops and lops from the oaks at Birkland. Do you suppose Samuel's father to have some involvement in the sale? He could, perhaps, provide us with some small supply.

William: James Walker's business is of no matter. The sale is of no matter. Petty things Sarah. Always petty things.

Mrs Billingsley: Oh, there are coals enough for your firings, no doubt. No matter anything else!

As if reminded of his work, Mr Billingsley leaves the living quarters and heads for the pottery area, sharply informing Mrs Sarah Billingsley, as he goes, that he will be gone until suppertime.

The elder of their two daughters, Sarah, is a little more sympathetic towards her father and tries to ease the growing tensions.

Sarah: Can I help you with the kneading today Mother? You look tired.

Mrs Billingsley: No thank you Sarah. I am really quite well. (*The dough is thrown down hard onto the table. She continues with this show of strength throughout the ensuing conversation.*) I don't know why your father must be so obstinate. His painting at Derby was much admired – and his gilding wasn't easily bettered. We could live quite comfortably if we were to return to Derby, and I'm sure there would be no difficulty in his securing a position there.

Sarah: Mother, you know well his purpose. And how much better his painting will look upon his own, finer porcelain. It is the difficulty in achieving this that causes his ill temper. You must not mind it.

Mrs Billingsley: Oh yes. I do know well his purpose. It is a selfish purpose. What is to become of our daughters? Lavinia is little more than a child yet, but you Sarah – *she looks to her* – a grown woman of four and twenty. Who is going to take the daughter of a pauper for a wife? … Oh, I have noticed how attentive

Samuel is towards you, and he is a good man. But your father fills Samuel's head with the same notions that fill his own. The madness between them doubles faster than this dough!

Thomas Holland, cheeky apprentice to Samuel Walker, hears two pairs of footsteps crossing the pottery yard and pauses his moving of bricks to better listen to their conversation.

William: The new manufactory will do well with no need of the old iron muffle and oven Samuel. How do the plans go for your enamelling kiln?

Samuel: Well enough William.

Thomas calls over "Will there be more pots to add for oven tomorrow Mr Samuel Sir?" Samuel checks with William. William confirms that "Yes. There will be a firing."

Samuel: Did you hear that Thomas?

Thomas: Yes Sir. Is Mr Wells to pay us a visit soon Sir? I 'ear 'e's after a great number of wares from us. Bet 'e's feared of 'aving 'is things took again if 'e was to cum near 'ere. I 'eared 'e was robbed of a pair o' boots an' a silk 'ankerchief last time.

Samuel reminds Thomas that the thief had been apprehended and deported for seven years. He jokes with Thomas that he will be joining him if he doesn't get on with his work. Thomas laughs, but William does not share the jovial mood.

William: Come on Samuel. Leave the lad and his nonsense; we've serious matters to discuss. Things are progressing so slowly, the debts are getting harder to meet and I need more wares promptly. We'll need to buy what we can't yet produce; Mr Wells is wanting views of Torksey, including ones of Brampton Pottery House and of the intended manufactory. A painting of the manufactory may be all of it that is achieved of it, it seems.

Inside the pottery house Samuel admires Sarah's work, which is on the less important pieces. Sarah thanks him, and quickly turns her attention to her father.

Sarah: I have the company of a young gentleman, come lately to the district from a brief employment at the Derby manufactory. He has brought some of his work to show you Father.

She moves to where the young man sits and indicates the plates in front of him. William's frustration is immediately obvious. He bangs a fist on the table, causing the pots to rattle, before thrusting said fist in front of the young man's eyes.

William: Look, look! Crude, worn out and useless as it is, even this fist has lights and shades, young sir. Can you not see them?

Samuel comes to the young man's assistance, and in a low voice advises, "Note you, young sir, the white of the knuckles as they resist the entry of red angry blood."
Meanwhile, William has picked up a plate and is giving it proper consideration.

William: You do not do your flowers justice, lad. Look harder. Where the light falls on a flower it will, of course, make that area of the flower paler, sometimes very much paler. But it would be quite astonishing if it were to transform it to the colour of the paste of the plate. So, do not make it so by omitting all colour on that spot. Give the flower its colour, and then remove as much of it as you need to, to show the true effect of light. The grouping is fair, but that too could be improved upon: use depth of colour to show position in the group, to give a better perspective, make clear which is the nearer. ... You will find others happy to give you employment, no doubt. We cannot.

William Billingsley struggles on with his Brampton-in-Torksey manufactory for some months, but the financial position does not improve. Every day something more is needed to be bought; new benefactors are sought and old creditors avoided. A crisis point is reached.

William: Preparation of supper can wait a little Sarah. We need to speak. I fear it can be left no longer.

Mrs Billingsley: Not even until after supper?

William: No. No longer! Will you please stop your work and listen to me. Our situation is desperate. In short, you must be prepared for us to leave Brampton before next Lady Day.

Mrs Billingsley: Are you finally come to your senses? Are we to return to Derby?

William: Never Sarah. Never. Derby has no interest in my improved porcelain now Mr Duesbury is dead, and so I have no interest in that manufactory. But, the Messrs Barr and Mr Flight at Worcester may be persuaded to think differently. I have high hopes of it.

Mrs Billingsley: But why must we move again? If you are still of the same stubborn mind as always; if you must spend every penny on clay and coal, why not do it here, produce your porcelain here, at Brampton?

William: You know well the difficulties we have long been under Sarah. Tomorrow, Bankes will be adjudged bankrupt; he owes money to Wells and to Walker. Neither they, nor anyone I know here, will be capable of advancing sufficient capital to build, or to redeem all of the debts. Many are in my name and I will be pursued for them if we stay. We will fare much the better elsewhere.

The Billingsleys have been at Brampton for four years. The move there was the third – Pinxton and Mansfield in between – since the twenty or so years of settled life they had spent in Derby, the settled life for which Mrs Sarah Billingsley now grieves. The despair she had felt when first William had been obliged to sell the 'Nottingham Arms', property bequeathed to him by his father, returns now with a vengeance. She speaks to her daughter thus.

Mrs Billingsley: No more Sarah. I will not run away to live amongst strangers and depend on their charity. We will go back to Derby, to your grandmother's house, for a time. When your father is in a position to secure us a home, we will go to it. If he decides instead to join us in Derby and take up a position there, I will not object. … But we cannot be subjected to such humiliation that will attend us if we wander with your father, Sarah: the dread that our creditors might apprehend us. For what should become of us then? We must go back to Derby Sarah and leave your father to his ways.

Sorry though Sarah is at the thought of being separated from her mother, her decision is instant. She conveys that decision as gently as she is able.

Sarah: Grandmother will manage your company happily Mother; a greater number would be burdensome. Besides, I can be of use to Father. I know it. I will be well protected Mother, for Samuel Walker is to be of our party. You need have no concerns on our behalf.

Lavinia is distraught at such consequences; her sister has always managed to reassure her and to soothe their mother through the worst of times. But times are changed.

This girl of eleven has to choose between going to Derby with her mother, or to somewhere unknown, with her father.

It is clear to Lavinia that Sarah will not desert Father. And if this means a parting from her dear sister, then Lavinia cannot desert Father either.

Life at Brampton has been far from ideal, but further uncertainty is beyond Mother's tolerance. Separation of mother and daughters is inevitable.

After Mother's initial sobbing; her repeated conviction that she will not see any of them again; and declarations that the situation is unbearable, the intense pain for all continues, but is now silent; masked with practicalities and distractions.

William: A case, containing a great quantity and variety of china, is to be sent to Derby. Take heed Sarah. We have not sufficient with which to clear our debts, but you may find occasion to part with these goods discreetly, and to good advantage. There will be difficulties to overcome in our contact with you if we are to avoid being prevailed upon by our creditors. This I know you understand and I know you will be patient in your expectations of monies from me.

Mrs Billingsley: You need have no concern of my expectations William. It saddens me that I know well enough what I can expect. (*She makes a show of rustling the newspaper she has in hand.*) I see in the 'Nottingham Journal' that James Walker has offered a guinea reward for the return of Thomas Holland. Shall I read the notice to you?

William: As you will Sarah.

Mrs Billingsley: "Run away: Thomas Holland, apprentice to Samuel Walker, stonemason and china manufacturer of Torksey. Holland is now aged about 21, 5ft 6ins high, stout made, light brown hair, marked with smallpox. Is impertinent in manner. Then wore dark blue coat, striped Manchester waistcoat, and light corduroy breeches. Believed to be in Derby area. Reward 1gn. Contact James Walker & sons, builders and farmers of Nottingham." (*Sarah again rustles the newspaper as she discards it.*) I think the guinea best kept in the pocket and Holland best left wherever he chooses. Though, I can see no reason why Thomas Holland should be thought to be in the Derby area. William? Why is it supposed so?

William: Samuel and I suppose it so, because Holland knows that Derby is the one place we will not go. If you come across him Sarah you must be sure to let James Walker know. If not stopped, Holland may pass on some details of Samuel's new kiln …but, in truth, he has not the wit to understand its advantages.

The departure from Brampton is quickly executed; Mr and Mrs Billingsley are become well practised in the art of such flits.

As the group separates from Mrs Billingsley, many voices speak hurriedly over each other. Mrs Sarah Billingsley's and her daughter Sarah's are the most distinct … "Take care not to forget me. Be sure to write me often and look after little Lavinia". "I will Mother. I will. Goodbye".

Lavinia does not speak. She prefers to stand away. When her mother moves close, and hugs and kisses her, Lavinia squeezes her favourite locket, held tightly in her hand. But she does not speak.

The group, comprising William Billingsley, Samuel Walker, Sarah and Lavinia Billingsley, go first to Worcester.

Mr Martin Barr, one of the proprietors of the manufactory there, listens with great interest but is unable to offer employment. The manufactories at Caughley and at Bristol are also approached for a possible opening. There is none.

William refuses to consider a return to Derby, and remains optimistic; the manufactories in South Wales are a worthy option, he believes. The group board, at Bristol, a ship bound for Wales.

None of this bunch of travellers is accustomed to travel by water and each one is inconvenienced by a great storm that comes upon them. Sarah fares much the worst.

Sarah groans: Mother! Oh Mother! I fear you were right when you said we would not see each other again. How many months will you wait to hear from me, not knowing that I am dead? You will never read of it; not of the death of Sarah Billingsley, for we dare not go by our own name. Oh Mother, that I had never stepped onto this ship!

Meanwhile, her father speaks with another passenger of his concerns for his daughter, Sarah, who has been violently ill for the last eight hours and has little strength left.

The passenger is a stranger, but obligingly shares his experience with William: "I have made this journey many times before and known many a storm, but none as severe as this. We are now near to Newport. Respite will be sought in the harbour there, before going on to Swansea. Hopefully, your daughter will regain her health sufficiently to continue."

But the plan fails. When it comes time to board ship for Swansea, Sarah refuses to do so.

William: Come now, my dear daughter. A short journey by ship will cause you no distress. Be assured of it and go to a cabin straight away, if that would content you.

Sarah: I wish I could do as you ask Father, but I cannot. I fear I would not survive the journey even if we were to have the calmest of waters. For I feel so ill at the sight of the ship, my feet cannot move though I will them to do so.

William: Look away from the ship Sarah. Think yourself out for a stroll. I will guide you.

Sarah: I cannot.

William: Come now Sarah. There is no alternative. You are not strong enough to walk the miles to Swansea and we have not the means to pay for a coach. We must board ship.

Sarah: I am trying. I am trying. But I cannot.

Samuel: Sarah. You always find it easier to think of others than to consider yourself. Think now of your sister Lavinia. Would you make it impossible for her to sail too? Would you make her walk such a distance? For none of us will board without you.

Sarah: Forgive me Lavinia. I would that I could! But look how the illness takes me and makes me shake. And the beast that would kill me still 500 yards from us.

It is true that Sarah is quite changed in her appearance; white and shivering as though dressed in ice, yet water running from her face as though it were melting from the heat.

Not one dares to question her reason further. They cannot board ship. They must walk to Swansea.

Suffice it to know of the journey that it is to be more than fifty miles; they have little money to eat fittingly for such exertion, and the trials can be well imagined without further description.

Once at Swansea, William wastes not a minute in seeking out Mr Dillwyn, proprietor of the manufactory. He is most anxious to report of his new porcelain and does so enthusiastically. However, William finds that a Mr William Weston Young, a decorator of pottery and also assistant to Mr Dillwyn, is much the more receptive of the two and, once again William is disappointed. Mr Young does not have the means and Mr Dillwyn does not have the inclination.

With this final rejection, they have no way of earning and are almost destitute, when a visitor from Worcester seeks out William. He has a message from Mr Barr that there is now an opening at Worcester manufactory!

Sarah writes to her mother with the news:

October 24th 1808

My Dear Mother,

We are again in our native country, after experiencing very great hardships. There were no openings in Swansea and we were quite desperate until Mr Barr sent word that there was an opening, and sent a small advance to help our return. Father has got into his situation as promised, but wages are very low for a good hand. Indeed he has not more at present than the common hands, but is given opportunity for experiments to improve the Worcester porcelain body. Lodgings and house rent is uncommonly dear. We pay 6s a week for two rooms, and they are reckoned the cheapest rooms in town. Every cost is so high and Father's wages so low, that with every frugality we could not subsist on it, and now Lavinia and myself have begun to go to work. It is not burnishing. It is work you never saw, a new type of printing. You may judge of the low wages when I tell you that when first burnishing, of which you know, not more than 3s 6d a week can be earned here, and no matter how many years of work after, never more than 6s a week. Samuel has not got a situation yet but is promised one soon. I am afraid you will hardly be able to make out all of my letter. Indeed, I can hardly see what I have written my eyes ache so with looking at work all day. Do be very particular in observing if the seal of this letter is safe. I will, in my next, say all the particulars of where we are. Father and Lavinia join in love to you and Grandmother. Samuel desires his best respects to you. Adieu my dear mother and believe me your very affectionate,

Sarah B.

It is not too long before Samuel is able to advise Sarah that when she writes next to her mother she may tell her that he has secured a position.

Samuel: You may guess what work it is to be Sarah. I am to build a kiln at Worcester in the manner of the one we hoped to have at Brampton. The Messrs Barr and Mr Flight are, all three of them, cautious men, but yet I sense a strong desire in the senior Mr Barr to have the beautiful porcelain we promise: the new white gold. Yes, it will be a new white gold Sarah. Your father makes good progress on the paste he produced at Pinxton and Brampton. We shall reach perfection.

As well as simple work at the manufactory, Lavinia helps with domestic tasks, but it is her sister who takes the brunt and will not admit to the tiredness that has dogged her ever since the trauma of their journey.

Samuel carries out his work during the night and so Sarah sees quite little of him. Despite this, the affection between the two grows.

It is 1812, almost four years after their arrival in Worcester, when they marry: a happy occasion, but both Sarah and Lavinia feel a sadness at the absence of their mother. Wages remain low and they are able to save too small an amount for them yet to be re-united.

Mr Martin Barr moves further towards adopting the new porcelain. This gives them hope.

Martin Barr: I am pleased with your results William. The paste is undoubtedly superior to our standard soaprock. But it will not do until the problem of wastage is properly addressed.

William: It needs only minor adjustments. Samuel and I judge that it will take some further experimentations, but we can improve the stability in the firing.

Martin Barr: I certainly hope so. This is a very costly business. If we are to continue we must be certain that it will be this manufactory, and only this manufactory that will have the benefit. It is time now William that you made your formula known to us. I will pay, to you and Samuel, the sum of £200 in exchange for the formula and full details of its production. In addition, I require that you William, and Samuel enter into a bond of £1000; the formula and method of production shall not be used to the profit of any partners, or yourselves if engaged with other partners. I must insist on your signatures to this.

William does not agree to sell ownership of his formula. However, he does make one concession.

William: I thank you for your confidence in my porcelain Sir. If the bond is clear in its wording, that Samuel and I are permitted to produce the porcelain – which is, and will remain, our own porcelain – whenever and wherever we wish, so long as we do not have other partners in the venture, then we will sign.

Thus, the secret of the formula is retained by William but the bond is duly agreed, signed – on November 17th 1812 – and work carries on.

Although some fine pieces are produced, the disappointments are numerous. The more adventurous the modelling, the more useless it is to be found after firing. And then, almost a year to the date from the agreement, Mr Martin Barr dies. This has dire consequences for William and Samuel.

Martin Barr's successors are unwilling to proceed with William's porcelain, and yet are afraid that competitors may be more willing to take the risk. And be successful.

William and Samuel are reminded of the bond in the severest manner. They are advised that there will be no hesitation to prosecute and demand the £1000 if the bond is broken.

Once again, William becomes dissatisfied with his position.

William: Almost five years I work for them. Still they pay me little more than common hands, and tie my own into the bargain! What are we to do next Samuel? My poor Sarah is quite worn down. It is too hard for her to see you leave for your work when she has barely returned from her own.

Samuel: Do not attempt to blame Sarah's ill health on my work William. If I had worked in daylight, all would have known details of the kiln before darkness fell. And it is done now. The kiln is completed. Even the young Barr is overjoyed with the result. The uniform heat we get from the side coals improves the general firing a great deal … though it is the improvement in costs, not porcelain, that pleases Barr so well. No, William. There is no resentment in Sarah. She shares completely in the joy of my success.

William: As I do Samuel. Indeed I do. The reason for my ill temper, if so it seems to you, is the refusal of young Barr to use my paste in production. You have seen its whiteness, its excellent translucency. It cannot be bettered – when all goes well in the firing.

Samuel: Therein lies the problem for Mr Barr – 'when all goes well in the firing'. He will not risk the loss of nine plates to get one good.

William: The 'one good', as you say, is far better than good Samuel. It is perfection. He cannot see that, and therein lies the problem for Barr!

Samuel: It is true that Barr can see profit more readily than perfection. And that is the problem for us. But we cannot go to another manufacturer; one for whom the joy of perfection is all – if one such manufacturer exists. We cannot because we have sworn and signed that we will not.

William and Samuel begin to work surreptitiously to secure the means by which they could gain the freedom to leave Worcester and produce their precious porcelain.
Progress is slow, until a most expedient, though unexpected, meeting happens between William and the Mr Young with whom William had spoken previously in Swansea. William tells something of their current position, to which Mr Young responds.

Mr Young: Then it is timely that we should meet, though I admit to it being of no coincidence. I had occasion to examine a plate of your new paste but a month ago. It was a fine piece. Am I correct in assuming that, because of the position you have described, if you were to leave Worcester to produce your porcelain elsewhere, you would be tormented by Barr to return, for fear you would make gains for a competitor?

William: That is so. Do you have a solution to our problem Mr Young?

Mr Young: I believe I do. If you were to receive money from me, enough to build a small kiln or two, would you and your family be willing to move to Nant-Garw? It is an isolated place near to Cardiff. There is no pottery there, so it should not occur to anyone to seek you out in such a place.

William: There will be other expenses to meet, besides the cost of kilns – coals, materials for the paste and so forth. I trust these can be taken care of until production is established?

Mr Young agrees all in principle. It should be carefully noted that William Billingsley has not been totally honest with Mr Young; he has not made him familiar with the detail of the £1000 bond.

It means another flit – to the Welsh hills. Secrecy is essential, to avoid arrest. They move under darkness and under the name of Beeley.

As usual, it is left to Sarah to inform her mother of the plans. And as Sarah is again unwell, and must adhere to strict instruction not to be too explicit, the letter is not an easy task.

November 9th 1813

My dear Mother,

I am glad to hear you are in good health. It will not be too long, I hope, before I can write to say I am the same, but for the present I am still suffering from an illness and, therefore, will save some telling of trivial news, which might entertain you, until I have more strength. Most things here remain the same as always. There is a general want of money to carry on Father's improvement in porcelain. And, as always, his endless passion for such things has excited others to a similar passion. In some ways he is a prisoner at Worcester and looks for ways out of this difficulty. Our position may soon be similar to what it was before, when we left Brampton and journeyed from Worcester to South Wales. If you have difficulty in understanding my meaning, you may attribute the confused words to my fever. Though, I judge you may understand me, and Father, well enough.

I am too tired to write more today. Lavinia, Father, and my dear husband Samuel join in love to you and Grandmother, and respects to all in Derby who still remember us.

Your very affectionate Sarah W.

(My dear Mother, it seems you often have to get used to changes in name!)

Two firing kilns (one for biscuit, the other for enamelling) are promptly erected at Nant-Garw and work begins.

But, once again, a similar story ensues; funds are exhausted before favourable conditions for the stability of the paste have been realized. Mr Young is bankrupt within a year. However, so strong is his belief in the porcelain that he prevails upon Mr Dillwyn to extend his pottery works at Swansea to accommodate William and Samuel and enable them to continue the development of their porcelain. And so impressed is Mr Dillwyn with the good specimens from Nant-Garw, that he agrees.

Success is close. All might yet have been well, but for the discovery by the proprietors of Worcester of the whereabouts of William and Samuel.

Whether it was Sarah's letter to her mother indicating the move to Wales; whether Thomas Holland heard rumours around Derby; or whether it was by some other means that they were discovered, we do not know. But a letter from Barr and his partners confirmed the knowledge. It was addressed to Samuel and he read aloud a portion of it.

You and Mr Billingsley are jointly and severally bound to us to forbear from communicating the secret to any person or persons whomsoever. We now inform you of our firm resolution to instantly give our attorney Instructions to Commence an Action against you for the amount of Penalty of one Thousand Pounds named in the Bond given to us the 17th day of November 1812.

We are Sir, Yrs etc. Flight, Barr & Barr.

P.S. We shall await the return of the Post for your answer before we address a Letter on this subject to Mr Dillwyn.

No answer is sent and Mr Dillwyn duly receives the letter Flight, Barr and Barr have threatened to send. William and Samuel discuss the consequences.

William: Dillwyn is such a weak man: a word from Barr and he so easily withdraws his support for my porcelain. Though before he keenly expressed such an appreciation of its qualities.

Samuel: I think you speak of him unjustly William. He was astonished to learn of our clandestine departure from Worcester, but still his manner remains quite gentleman-like. Some might argue our conduct has not been so. I fear we must accept his instruction to cease further experiments with our formula, and we must try a new one, with more soaprock. We should easily make one that is more stable in the firing and it may prove to be acceptable, even to you William.

William: If we are to eat, then we must. But Dillwyn need not expect to have the quality of our Nant-Garw wares.

Such it carries on for two years. A changed formula is used, and wastage is reduced as expected. But, as William predicted, the Swansea porcelain, though good, does not have the same translucency as that of Nant-Garw and does not sell so easily.

Mr Dillwyn tires of the venture and takes the decision to close down the china part of his works.

Mr Young, the ever-loyal friend, although without means, takes it upon himself to show the Nant-Garw specimens to many local business and tradesmen. Before too long, he interests a number of such acquaintances in providing sufficient help for a return to the kilns at Nant-Garw.

Samuel is not anxious to go immediately. He does not want to be idle in Nant-Garw when he can be useful in Swansea, and sees reason to wait a little until matters are settled in Nant-Garw. He asks Sarah for her thoughts on this proposition.

Sarah: I do not think too much of any particular place Samuel. I think only of wherever our circumstances can be improved. If Lavinia does not object to making the arrangements in Nant-Garw, then I shall be pleased to stay here a while longer. I think I would be the better for taking some rest. And I think rest can be better taken here.

The separation is to be short, but Lavinia misses Sarah greatly. Again, we are reminded that through all the times of uncertainty, Sarah has been her sole comfort.

Generally, it is only Sarah who takes the trouble to write to their mother. But, shortly after Lavinia and her father arrive in Nant-Garw, Lavinia is obliged to undertake such a task: the most terrible of tasks.

On the first of January 1817 Lavinia writes the letter she must write. She never writes again.

The next letter to Mrs Billingsley is written by William:

September 8th 1817
My dear wife, Sarah,
My sufferings are now arrived at the highest pitch of misery. I lost on the 1st of January my dear elder daughter Sarah, which my dearest Lavinia wrote to you, on the day, to tell of the event. But, I have scarce calmed a little my feelings for the loss of dear Sarah, than dearest Lavinia is taken from me.

The dearest child was taken ill last Monday morning with a violent pain in her stomach. In violent pain she continued on Saturday and Sunday. On the Sunday evening (yesterday), she was suddenly worse. This morning, to my inconsolable grief, I found all hope of recovery was at an end. She died in my presence at a little before one o'clock this day, to enjoy everlasting bliss above, leaving me a distressed mortal, never more to be happy.

I wish I had means to send for you. I have none. My difficulties here are great; my success uncertain for want of a little money but my loss is greater in my dearest young Lavinia. She was my only stay and comfort. I can write no more.

Remaining your afflicted and affectionate, William Beeley.

◇◇◇

All around her the auction bids come fast and furious. Lavinia listens not to the numbers. She is overwhelmed as her father's plate is held aloft for the buyers to see.

She wants to be closer. She rushes up to the porter.

There is not one person in the crowd who does not shiver as Lavinia passes: calling

"Mother, my dear mother. What do you think now?

"The plate is a treasure. White gold.

"Do you see Mother? Do you see?"

Introduction to Group II

◇◇◇

This group focuses on investigations stemming from my interest in antique ceramics. An interest acquired from frequent browsing of items for sale at Tennants Auction House in Leyburn. (Visits to Tennants were solely for a meal initially. It was my reward for rising at the crack of dawn to accompany my husband to the gallops at nearby Middleham. The wonderful sight of racehorses against the backdrop of the Yorkshire Dales was almost enough to get me out of bed in all weathers: but not quite.)

I must stress at the outset that I am not an expert in ceramics. Over the years I have picked up on some snippets: for instance, I understand that porcelain, the most prized ceramic body, is fired at a high temperature and is generally translucent; earthenware is fired at a lower temperature and, although it can be potted thinly, it generally remains opaque – descriptions are sometimes given according to the glaze applied (creamware, unsurprisingly, has a cream glaze, pearlware has a blue tinged glaze); stoneware is fired at the lowest temperature and is both opaque and porous. Further refinements associated with different recipes of the paste and other variables I leave to the ceramic specialists.

However, it is worth remembering that porcelain was produced in China centuries before Europe was able to discover the secret (hence the ceramic term 'china'). And the struggle by Europeans to make this 'white gold' is part of the fascinating story of ceramics.

Amateur sleuthing has the enjoyment of discovery of a different nature. All the information I present is out there for anyone to find and tends to centre on people, prompted by pots.

Books, Internet, conversations and observations, all play a part in building up the picture, but it is crucial to recognize when and how to verify points of significance.

The Mystery of Thomas Mason was my first article to do with ceramics. The idea unfolded gradually as I read, searched for clues and read some more, until I was bursting to write down how it all came together.

At that time, I did not know of any ceramic interest groups and decided to offer my writing for publication in *Antiques Magazine*. I was thrilled that it was accepted (published in issue 945, 14th-20th December 2002). Not so thrilled when I read how it had been introduced. *Pam Gardiner investigates the mystery of Thomas Mason, and comes up with some shocking – and controversial – conclusions.* And at the end asked *Convinced? Appalled?* (I was relieved that my name had a spelling error. Perhaps no one would identify me.)

But I was not lynched. I now understand that *shocking* sells copy; *controversy* sells copy; collectors may be *appalled* by ripples that unsteady their precious cargo.

By 2005 I was a member of 'The Northern Ceramic Society' (NCS). The article was re-published and I was excited to hear from author Vega Wilkinson that I had *put Thomas Mason on the map.*

Since then I have published many other articles in the NCS Newsletter. *Have You Seen This Woman?* and *Thurot vs. Tito* come from amalgamations of research carried out for such articles.

Have You Seen This Woman? is a good example of how earlier findings can contribute massively to solving new, seemingly impossible puzzles.

I spent five years studying connections to a William Weston who had commissioned a porcelain service in the early 1800s (which culminated in the book *Billingsley, Brampton and Beyond – In search of The Weston Connection,* published by Troubador in 2010). The Westons proved to have links with Jane Austen's family.

It was useful then, and continues to be so in the placing of protagonists; the extended and extensive families of Jane Austen are the more easily researched because of her fame, and have, on occasions, become something of a shorthand way of identifying broader circles of acquaintances. This is one of those occasions.

Thurot vs. Tito brings together historical events in a surprising manner: one that provides for me a seemingly inexhaustible source of intrigue.

The last in this group, *Was Miriam Weston of Sound Mind?* is slightly different; it does not in itself revolve around any ceramic piece. It is, however, an aside from an investigation into the provenance of the Weston porcelain service, referred to previously.

Thanks are owed to friends, family and fellow writers who read through this section and advised on accessibility to readers who may have no interest in ceramics. In particular to: Linda Bradshaw; Maggie Cobbett; Dave Gardner; Steve Gardner; Glyn Myerscough; Zara Peermohamed; and Vicki Yates.

The Mystery of Thomas Mason

◇◇◇

Who is Thomas Mason? He is the man behind the signature on the exquisite, white enamelled, Minton vase, which dates to between 1891 and 1901 (figures 1,2).

There appears to be little evidence of his existence, other than his signature is occasionally found on Minton pieces. Why is this?

Consider the following facts.

Mason's work was sufficiently admired by Colin Minton Campbell (a one-time Director of the Minton factory) to form part of his personal collection, alongside the masters of ceramic decoration such as Solon, Birks (a student of Solon's) and Leroy (or Leroi, as he was known in France); Mason was permitted to sign his own work, a privilege not afforded to many; the factory's globe mark on the base of the featured vase is printed in gold (figure 3), a feature reserved especially for the best pieces.

The high quality of Mason's work is further evidenced by the fact that high prices were paid at auction for his work. Mr. C. Minton Campbell's ceramic collection was sold at Christie's auction house in 1902. Lot 34 was a pair of vases and covers

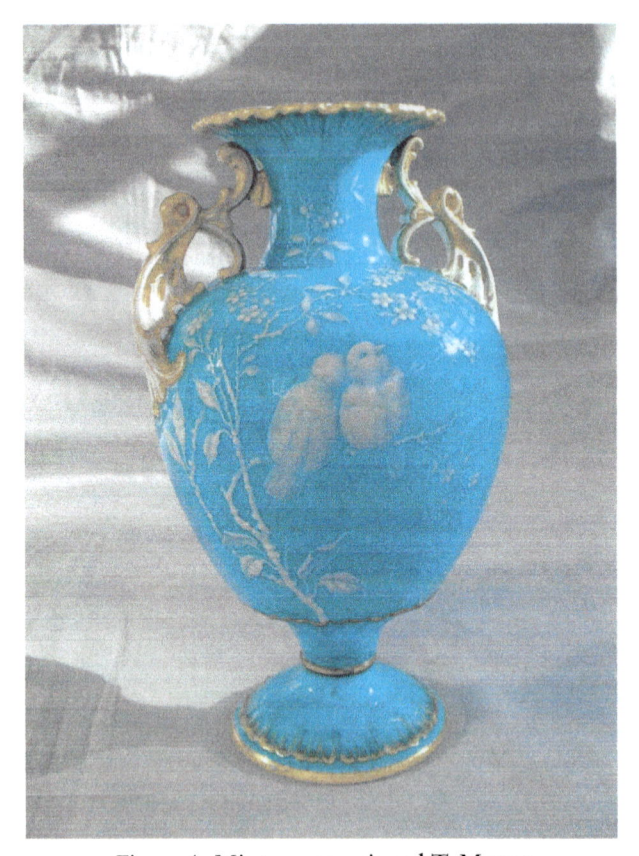

Figure 1. Minton vase, signed T. Mason

Figure 2. T. Mason signature

Figure 3. Mintons globe, in gold

... with figures and flowers in white ... on an olive-green ground by A. Birks. (Note that at this time, the description "in white" could refer to either of the techniques pâte sur pâte, or Limoges enamelling; more on this later.) Lot 35 was a pair of vases and covers described as *nearly similar* (to lot 34), *with dark blue ground* by Mason (figure 4).

The vases by Birks sold for £17/17/-; the 'nearly similar' ones by Mason sold for £24/3/-. (Note that the work of Solon – and that of Birks – was always highly rated, which makes it surprising that an 'unknown' Mason drew such interest. It suggests that Campbell and the buyers of 1902 were privy to some information that we do not have.)

Today, pieces by A. Birks still fetch extremely high prices, arguably second only to those by Solon himself. This ranking in value is worth emphasizing:

1902 – 1st Mason, 2nd Birks
Today – 1st Solon, 2nd Birks.

There is no record in the Minton Archive index of Thomas Mason. His name does not appear in the salary/wage books. All that is known is that he was active in the period 1870s –

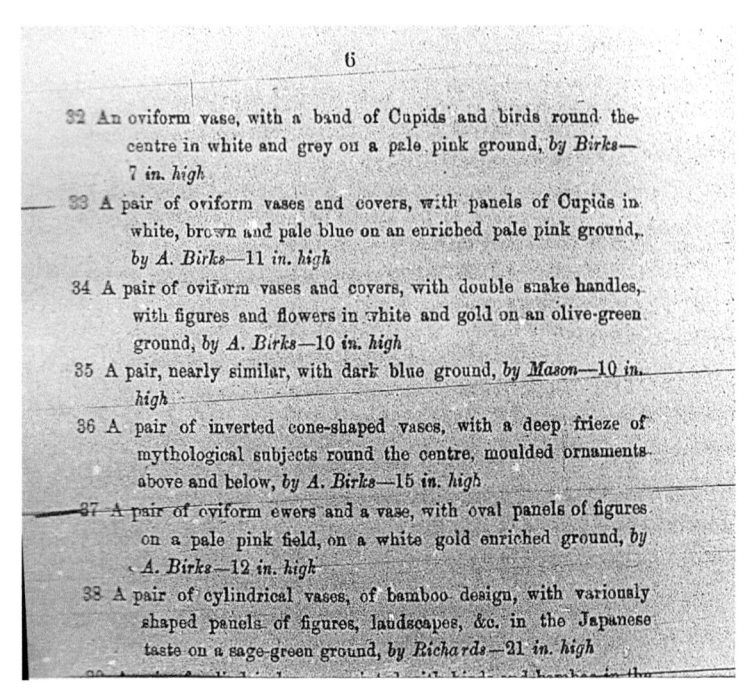

Figure 4. Entries from Christie's Auction Catalogue

1890s and specialized in the complex painting technique, Limoges enamelling, as on this vase.

Why so little information?

It is indeed a puzzle that nothing is known of so talented an artist whose work spanned such a long period.

The fire in the Kensington Art Pottery Studio in 1875, which destroyed some of Minton's records, would not account for the lack of information on Thomas Mason as the studio was used for decorating earthenware and had its own backstamp. In any case, the majority of Mason's work was carried out after this date.

However, there is one explanation for this puzzle. Thomas Mason did not exist. *Thomas Mason was a pseudonym*, used by Solon, who also worked for Minton from 1870s to 1890s (1870 – 1904).

Before I expand on my reasoning, it is necessary to give a little background information on Solon and the technique of which he was master.

Solon, 1835-1913, was born in France and worked at the Sèvres factory where he developed the decorating technique of pâte sur pâte (paste on paste). This is the painting of designs onto a coloured porcelain ground using successive layers of white liquid clay (slip).

In 1870 he left France for England and joined the workforce of the Minton factory; the Franco-Prussian war and Colin Minton Campbell each instrumental in the move. The relationship between C. Minton Campbell and Solon remained strong throughout their lives.

The standing of Solon within the world of ceramics was exceedingly high: a scholar; an author; and talented artist with an extraordinary flair for design, which sometimes incorporated his renowned sense of humour.

In 1894 Solon wrote an article for "The Studio", keen to distinguish the quality of pâte sur pâte from other methods of decoration, including Limoges enamelling, with which it was described:

> *A Pâte sur Pâte bas-relief … is always an original; a repetition of it could only be made by the artist who executed the first one. In the Limoges enamels, sometimes mentioned as presenting some analogy, the difference is … marked, for in this case effect is not obtained by gradations of relief, but rather of lights and shades. The dark tint of the ground is taken advantage of to form the shadows,*

and the white enamel comes into play, just as white chalk interferes in an effective drawing on tinted paper.

It should be added that the layering of slip is a painstakingly slow process. Care has to be taken to wait until one coat is perfectly dry before applying another. The layers are then worked into with sharp tools to perfect the details of the design.

Unsurprisingly, pâte sur pâte pieces are generally of higher value than enamelled pieces; note again the unusual ranking of Mason's enamelling above the pâte sur pâte of Birks at the 1902 auction.

And now we return to the puzzle.

Why use a pseudonym?

We know that Solon was not averse to using pseudonyms. In France, in the early days of developing the pâte sur pâte technique he used his initials (**Marc Louis Emmanuel Solon**), added the letter I, and came up with MILES. (Incidentally, he was later to refer to Miles, the Staffordshire potter of around 1685, in his book *The Art of the Old English Potter*.) He was never precious about any one form of signature, variously using Miles, M. Miles, MLS, Solon, L. Solon, M.L. Solon, and M. Solon-Miles. One vase, with a figure of a Japanese girl, he marked with a pseudo-Japanese monogram.

White enamelling is not the mode of decoration on which Solon had built his considerable reputation, so it is not inconceivable that he would enjoy employing a new pseudonym for work that would not be expected from him.

Solon referenced the close relationship he had with C. Minton Campbell in an inscription to him in an edition of the book referred to previously: ... *If the author of this imperfect essay presumes to dedicate it to you, it is only as a tribute of personal respect, and an acknowledgment, however inadequate, of many favours received at your hands.*

One such favour was the permission for Solon to sometimes work at home. But the personal notebook that Solon kept to record information whilst at Minton did not include details of this work.

In 1901 Solon noted that many of his MILES pieces had made their way to England, which he regretted as, in some, their shortcomings were evident. Perhaps this is an indication that he was not as random in his choice of signature as might appear.

Why choose Thomas Mason as a name?

Thomas means twin. Mason's work has 'twinned' other work on at least two occasions:

1. The Christie's catalogue of 1902 described the Mason vases as "nearly similar" to the previous lot by A. Birks. (A reminder that Birks decorated in pâte sur pâte – he was a student of Solon's. Mason achieved "nearly similar" vases by enamelling. Quite a challenge.)
2. The birds on our Mason vase are unmistakably in the style of birds painted in white enamel by Leroy. (Leroy, like Solon, left France for England and worked at Minton). This is the work for which Leroy is perhaps best known and respected.

Thomas, therefore, chose two of the best artists of the time (excepting Solon) to emulate.

MASON as a choice of name is obvious. It can be so easily derived from **MA**rc Sol**ON**.

But, there is an extra twist to this conjecture. Miles Mason was a known Staffordshire potter (distinct from the Miles of

1685), who made 'copying' respectable. This is a quote from an advertisement by Mason's in the *Morning Herald*, 1804 on the subject of reproducing china from other lands: *Being aware that, to combat strong prejudices with success, something superior must be produced ... he proposes ... to match ... the broken pieces of the nobility ... when, by a fair trial ... he ... will rival, if not excel, those of foreign nations.*

Having previously used MILES, his amusement in coming up with MASON can well be imagined.

Having put forward a case for Thomas Mason being a pseudonym, I shall now adopt the null hypothesis, this generally being the easiest to prove. So, Thomas Mason is not Marc Solon. The challenge now is to prove he is not.

Part Two: The Challenge

I have Northern Ceramic Society member Ernie Luck to thank for his response to part one of this saga, and for the information he shared (in 2006. Later research is now also included).

The census of 1881 shows as many as one hundred and eleven Thomas Masons in Staffordshire. But from all the occupations given, only one is a possibility for the Thomas Mason at Minton. If the signature is not a pseudonym, then this has to be our man.

Below outlines some key points:

- 1871 census – painter (aged 15 years old)
- 1881 census – potter flower painter
- 1891 census – flower painter
- 1901 census – potter's painter
- 1911 census – flower painter (earth)

- He married Annie Rebecca Hancock in 1877 at which time he moved from his parents home at Shelton, Stoke-upon-Trent to Newcastle-under-Lyme. Two further addresses are recorded, both in Stoke-upon-Trent. Minton is in the vicinity (along with many other contemporary factories).
- The signature of Thomas Mason on his marriage certificate does not match that on the vase. There are several notable differences that make it impossible to say these are the signatures of the same man. However, the differences may be due to such things as the lapse of time, a different medium and/or the difference in occasion.
- In three of the five census returns Thomas Mason describes himself specifically as a painter of flowers, yet the main subjects on at least two of the few known pieces are birds and figures.

And, of course, there remains the fact that Thomas Mason does not appear in Minton factory records. It is not unknown for records of artists to be missing. Though, for reasons given earlier, it is most surprising that this artist is not properly recorded.

To my knowledge, no 'Mason' signed, enamelled pieces dating later than 1901 have emerged, yet we know the flower painter Thomas Mason was still working in 1911.

We still have no evidence to tell us at which factory (or factories) the Thomas Mason, born circa 1855, was employed. Records for the smaller Staffordshire factories are scant.

Research continues, but for the present we have not met the challenge; we have not been able to rule out the possibility that Thomas Mason may be a pseudonym for Marc Solon.

Have You Seen This Woman?

◇◇◇

The sitter for the portrait on the illustrated porcelain coffee can, dating to the early 1800s, is unnamed. The purpose of this investigation is to identify her.

A possible clue, though it may be a red herring, comes from the knowledge that the can was once sold at auction (in 2012) as part of a lot that included some pieces from a porcelain service that had previously (in 2006) been researched by a member of the Northern Ceramic Society, Kenneth Hancock.

He had established that Anne Rushout of Northwick Park had painted the scenes on the service pieces.

This is my starting point.

If the 'can lady' is a self-portrait, then she most likely is not Anne; a pen and ink drawing by Henry Bone of Anne and her two sisters, Harriet and Elizabeth, do not show a distinguishable likeness. Two portraits of Anne – with powdered hair – by Andrew Plimer show no obvious likeness either, though not quite as easily dismissed.

Figure 1. Portrait on a porcelain can

However, it is interesting that Henry Bone comes on the scene – he was the father of Charles Francis Bone who sadly died at the age of 15, and whose likeness was enamelled in the early 1800s by ceramic artist Thomas Baxter.

We meet Thomas Baxter again later. But first, we return to Henry Bone, and more importantly to the significance of his note on the drawing:

The daughters of Lady Northwick
For Bowles Esq re Augst 1809

Figure 2. Plate decorated by Julia Leigh

Figure 3. Plate decorated by Caroline Leigh

That the drawing was for *Bowles esq.* gives us two routes to Jane Austen's family, established in earlier research on the Weston porcelain service. (Some expansion on the connections is given at the end.)

The can; the Rushout service; and the Weston service date to a similar time. If the context of the lady on the can lies within the life of Anne Rushout, then the possibilities of her identity are endless.

It is perhaps pertinent to consider elements of Anne's life in a search for further clues.

Anne, although an amateur artist, had considerable talent that was not restricted to painting on ceramics. She was fortunate that her position in society allowed for the indulgence of amateur status.

It was a position shared by several other young ladies who painted on ceramics, with varying levels of ability. Figures 2 and 3 show plates painted by Julia Leigh and Caroline Leigh respectively. These, and others, come from the Stoneleigh Chattels Settlement, and a direct Jane Austen interest.

Stoneleigh had been in the hands of the Leigh family since 1561, when purchased (at first jointly with Sir Rowland Hill) from William Cavendish, but it changed to a different line in 1786. After legal battles, Stoneleigh later passed to the Gloucestershire side of the family, to James Henry Leigh.

His wife Julia is the artist's name on one of the plates; Caroline – the name on the other plate – is Caroline Eliza Leigh, the daughter of James Henry and Julia.

A Christie's auction catalogue, July 2006, says of the Leigh plates (twenty-two in all), *The styles and subjects relate strongly to the work of independent porcelain decorators such as Thomas Baxter of London and Thomas Pardoe of Bristol ...*

Jane Austen, cousin of James Henry Leigh, visited Stoneleigh in 1806.

She and her mother had been staying at Adlestrop, Gloucestershire, the then home of James Henry and his uncle, Rev. Thomas Leigh when, on hearing that the Gloucestershire Leighs were in line to inherit the contested Stoneleigh, Thomas made haste there. He took with him his guests, Jane and her mother. (It was rubbing salt into the wound somewhat, given that Mrs. Austen's brother, James Leigh-Perrot had been one of the other claimants to the estate.)

Julia's mother joined the party and Jane's mother wrote of her as *rather tormenting, tho' something amusing, and affords Jane many a good laugh*. Jane's own view is not represented in the letter. Though we do have something of Jane's view of Julia (Mrs Leigh) and her sister (Miss Twisleton), written by Jane to Cassandra in 1801. *I then got Miss Twisleton to look at; ... I have a very good eye at an adultress ... I fixed upon the right one from the first. – A resemblance to Mrs Leigh was my guide ... her face has the same defect of baldness as her sister's, & her features not so handsome; – she was highly rouged, & looked rather quietly & contentedly silly than anything else.*

Despite the highly flushed cheeks of our sitter, I think we look elsewhere for an identification.

Several pieces of the Anne Rushout service feature Daylesford House, as on the can in figure 4. Could this be significant?

Daylesford House has a long, interesting history but suffice it to say that at the time of Anne's service it was occupied by Warren Hastings. He too has an interesting history; his early career, in the employ of the East India Company took him to Bengal; he later was to become the first Governor General of India.

Figure 4. Daylesford House by Anne Rushout

Warren Hastings was the godfather of Jane Austen's first cousin Elizabeth (known initially as Betsy but later as Eliza), daughter of Philadelphia, and he ensured her financial security.

It is well documented that Hastings was a close family friend of both the Leigh family from childhood, and the Austens; Jane Austen's father, George (brother of Philadelphia) was tutor to his son, young George Hastings, when Warren Hastings was in India.

Tragically, young George died of diphtheria whilst in the care of George Austen and his wife Cassandra (Leigh). Warren Hastings was journeying back to England at the time and learnt of the tragedy on his arrival. Eliza later married Jane Austen's brother Henry – secondly, her first husband having been guillotined in France.

This confirms and extends links to Jane Austen's family, with an ever-increasing number of eligible females, but no likenesses have thus been found.

A trawl of portraits of females from the era is warranted.

A Positive Sighting?

Figure 5 (courtesy of Bonhams, UK) is a miniature, painted in oil on ivory. Allowing for a slight loss of paint on the can and its likely execution being by an amateur, a likeness to the miniature can be seen, particularly about the characteristic mouth; her hair and her style of dress (see figures 6 and 7).

The miniature is of Susannah Smith (nee Mackworth-Praed) and was painted by the British artist James Leakey

Figure 5. Susannah Smith by James Leakey.
Courtesy of Bonhams, UK

HAVE YOU SEEN THIS WOMAN?

Figure 6. A close-up of the portrait on the can

Figure 7. A close-up of James Leakey's portrait of Susannah Smith

(1775-1865). After two or three decades as a successful artist of various subjects – in addition to portraits – James Leakey gave up that career to become a preacher.

His subject in this instance, Susannah Smith, was the wife of Thomas Smith of Bersted Lodge.

It is of great significance, with respect to our 'can lady', that these Smiths were of Bersted Lodge; Anne Rushout painted Bersted Lodge when on a visit there – her diaries are held at the University of London. The 'watercolour, pen and black ink' of Bersted Lodge, figure 8, is held at, and reproduced courtesy of Yale Center for British Art, Paul Mellon Collection.

In summary, the watercolour adds further substance to a conclusion that the portrait on the can is that of Susannah Smith; Anne Rushout has familial links to the Austens, as does

Figure 8. Bersted Lodge by Anne Rushout

Note: Thomas Smith (Susannah's husband) was the brother of Joshua Smith of Erlstoke, whose daughter Augusta married Charles Smith of Sutton. Their daughter Emma married James Edward Austen (nephew of Jane Austen), who became Rev. James Edward Austen Leigh. The Austen/Leigh families connect to Westons.

Susannah Smith; Anne Rushout has been to (and painted) Bersted Lodge, the home of Susannah Smith; there is a likeness to the Leakey portrait of Susannah Smith; and the can was sold with pieces known to be painted by Anne Rushout.

Please note, we have probably identified the sitter but still do not know who painted the can.

It would be wrong to assume Anne; it is not of the same quality as her landscapes, but I have seen no portraits by her to indicate her competence, or otherwise, in that area.

Neither do I know whether Susannah herself, or many of her other guests, enjoyed this popular pastime of painting on ceramics.

Could the identification of the artist be the subject of a future detective story?

Notes on connections established in previous research

Anne Rushout's mother was Rebecca Bowles; Bowles and Weston families were connected; Thomas Baxter portrayed Emma Hamilton on several ceramic pieces. His acquaintance with Emma, and Horatio Nelson, flourished at the same time as that with Henry Bone, and as that of Nelson with John Julius Angerstein. Angerstein, in turn, was associated with Westons.

Thurot vs. Tito

◇◇◇

The pictured, Sèvres, porcelain vase, figures 1 and 2 (reproduced courtesy of Christie's, New York), was stumbled upon and caught my eye because of the similarity to the painting on a creamware saucer, figures 3 and 4.

I am intrigued by an idea of what the painting may be depicting. For this same, unusual scene, to appear on two totally different pieces suggests it may be representative of something in particular. And it is worth noting that, as far as I am aware, the scene does not appear on any other ceramic pieces.

The only clues to follow are the red flag, held by one of the figures, and the title given on the vase, *Terme de T.*

A red flag was the recognized symbol of privateers – a warning to other vessels not to resist – known in France as le Jolie Rouge (perhaps the source of the Jolly Roger, a straightforward corruption of the French phrase; or because of the red coat worn by a not so jolly 'pirate' called Barti. The precise etymology is open to debate. Other examples are available).

Figure 1. Sèvres vase.
Courtesy of Christie's, New York

Figure 2. Scene on the Sèvres vase

Privateers are sometimes looked on as being synonymous with pirates but the one of whom I am about to write undoubtedly had the backing of the French government; a true privateer: Francois Thurot, 1727 – 1760.

I believe the T on the Sevres vase could relate to Thurot.

A lot of writings about Thurot can be found and they concur on all the general points, but the veracity of particular details is, at times, difficult to establish. A short overview of the man and his career should suffice.

Thurot's first venture to sea, at age seventeen (on a vessel engaged in privateering) was as a surgeon – having been apprenticed to a surgeon in Dijon for only one year. He was captured but escaped and from then on he was on board as a 'sailor'; a very successful one; a captain before he was twenty. He apparently worked as a merchant captain for a while – a smuggling of goods between the Isle of Man and Ireland is reported – before becoming a privateer proper, during the Seven Years War between France and Britain. As a consequence of his great success, by 1759 Louis XV had put him in charge of a squadron of five ships.

The name of Thurot became legendary, and he had supporters further afield than France. Perhaps this was due to his reputation for fairness and honour above a wish to plunder. In Britain, there were additional considerations; although born in France, Thurot is believed to have married a Londoner, Sarah Smith; more importantly, his maternal grandfather, Captain O'Farrell, was an Irishman who had served in the Irish Brigade.

This brings me to *Terme de T*, written on the vase, across the stone on which the two men are standing.

In 1760, after a series of events that had reduced his initial troops by over half to around 600, Thurot landed at Carrickfergus, County Antrim; overpowered the garrison and took control of the castle. His main concern was to replenish

Figure 3. Creamware saucer

Figure 4. Scene on the creamware saucer

provisions in fear his men would perish from famine. Thurot offered not to take his captives back to France, nor to plunder Carrickfergus if the provisions were brought.

(Could this be the negotiation being depicted in the painting? The '*Terms of Thurot*'?)

But nothing was forthcoming and Thurot was unable to stop his hungry French troops from going into the town to pillage. They re-stocked and re-sailed. Thurot was killed shortly after when he came into battle with a British fleet off the coast of the Isle of Man. His death was mourned by the British as well as by the French.

I published – in the Northern Ceramic Society (NCS) Newsletter, March 2014 – my interpretation of the scene and asked members for alternative suggestions. Immediately, Derek Cutts kindly sent me one to explore; he suggested the title could relate to *Terme di Tito*. This I duly did explore, and am very grateful for the ensuing interest it provided.

Terme di Tito translates from the Italian as the 'Baths of Titus' and refers to the public (thermal) baths built on land previously taken over by Nero.

For the artistic relevance we must firstly go back to the building and development of Nero's 'Domus Aureus', or 'Golden House', still not fully completed when he died in 68 AD. The frescoes and murals were by the great artist Fabullus. (Could this be the source of 'fabulous'? The word was first used in English, in the 15th to 16th centuries to describe something of an astonishing nature – as of a fable.)

As Nero's grand development fell into ruins, it was built over and changed many times; a memorial to Titus was erected there and this helped preserve some remains.

In the fifteenth century the subterranean rooms and

passages (le grotte) of the Golden House were rediscovered. And in the eighteenth century there was a further revival in popularity of the style of the original decoration, much of which has survived.

Franciszek Smuglewicz was one of the people to survey and draw the scenes of the relics and copied the frescoes, murals and motifs (from which Marco Carloni did his engravings). These, in the 1770s, were published as *Vestigia delle Terme di Tito e loro Interne Pitture*. The picture, figure 5, is from that publication, and figure 6 an extract from that picture.

The extract shows three figures admiring the uncovered art, the title – as of the 1770s publication – is written on the stone in the forefront.

Figure 5. Vestigia delle Terme di Tito e loro Interne Pitture

Figure 6. Three figures near the stone bearing the picture's title

These are similarities to the scene on the French vase (the saucer has no writing) that certainly warrant attention.

Piranesi was an archeologist, architect and engraver, who sometimes worked alongside Smuglewicz. Figure 7 is one of his engravings with a striking similarity in structure of the arches to those on the Sèvres vase.

I revisited the story (published in the NCS Newsletter, March, 2015) and have continued to reflect.

Of no little importance are the *political aspects*, and a need to put the ceramic pieces into this context.

In 1759, the Sèvres porcelain factory came under the control of Louis XV, who was influenced greatly by Madame de Pompadour. She had long spoken of the great advantages the State would derive from the ownership and management of porcelain in the Saxon fashion. Edicts were issued, which forbade any making, decorating or selling of porcelain other than that by Sèvres.

There was an outcry from other manufacturers.

In 1766 a fresh decree was issued that allowed for porcelain to be produced elsewhere, so long as it was in imitation of

Figure 7. Engraving of a Smuglewicz picture

the Chinese; was decorated only in blue and white or a single colour; and with no figures or ornaments in alto-relievo (in relief, raised from the background).

Louis XV died in 1774 and was succeeded by Louis XV1. The new king continued ownership of Sèvres, but was faced with a growing competition from other factories, which were increasingly producing porcelain, and in 1784 he revived the edicts Louis XV had issued.

Again there was an outcry. Many factories requested a delay to the edict. They were given a year to complete orders and from then could continue producing if not using gold or copying Sèvres style, unless permission was expressly given.

In 1789 all such authorizations and monopolies were abolished as a result of the revolution. The liberty of industry was decreed.

The Sèvres vase bearing our scene of interest dates to 1774, of a form described as 'Griffes de Lyon'. According to Christie's auction house, the factory records of Sèvres note only eleven of this form having been produced, all between 1774 and 1778.

(I have not been able to ascertain the name of the artist but one possibility, a specialist in marine and military subjects, is Jean-Louis Morin. He was the son of an army surgeon and, coincidentally like Thurot, initially studied for that profession before enrolling at Sèvres. Murin was known for originality, for painting from his own sketches.)

It is more difficult to date the creamware saucer. The style is that of creamware in the late 1700s but may well have been produced at a later date; the factory/decorator's mark on the reverse of the saucer is not one I can find recorded. So, not a fake but, nevertheless, may not be quite what it purports to represent.

During the period of Sèvres monopoly much fine creamware was produced in place of porcelain (some factories producing porcelain actually described their products as creamware in order to avoid penalties).

Between the NCS publications (of 2014 and 2015), I learned of fresh excavations at Carrickfergus Castle.

The Belfast Telegraph reported in March 2014: *An archaeological excavation at Ireland's best-preserved Anglo Norman castle has been extended after the discovery of a secret tunnel.* Figure 8 shows the entrance to a tunnel leading under Carrickfergus Castle; figure 9 (reproduced courtesy of 'The Carrick Times) is The Great Hall to where the newly discovered tunnel led.

(Please note that the newly discovered tunnel is distinct from the later built tunnels near to the entrance of the Castle.

Figure 8. Tunnel entrance under Carrickfergus Castle

Figure 9. The Great Hall, Carrickfergus Castle.
Courtesy of *The Carrick Times*

The later tunnels are to be renovated and to feature as a public attraction.)

Also reported was the find of ceramics dating from medieval times onwards and including those from British and French origin.

Carrickfergus Castle was built around 1177 by John De Courci, and has played a strategic part in battles throughout history. Although John De Courci was an Anglo Norman knight, there is a Roman style to the external defences of the town, figure 10. Note the arch and vegetation above, not too dissimilar to that on our scene. (This image, on the Library of Ireland website, was taken from the *Dublin Penny Journal*, May 1833.)

Figure 10. North Gate Entrance to Carrickfergus

Finally, I return to the comparison of Thurot with Tito as possibilities for the 'T' on the vase.

The *Terme di Tito* pictures have arches/tunnels. Carrickfergus and its Castle too have similar constructs, if not as obvious.

One of the Italian pictures has three figures standing on stone bearing the title. The *Terme de T* vase features similar, though with two figures.

Here, we cannot overlook the fact that it is a French vase with French words that are particularly applicable to the scene; 'terme de' is commonly used in relation to agreements and, unlike in the Tito picture, the two figures are facing each other as if in conversation. There are no grounds for assuming a spelling error of de instead of di. Neither does the French scene indicate any rediscovered artwork, as would be pertinent if a representation of 'di Tito'.

Of less significance, but worth a mention is an alternative use of 'terme', to mean an ending of sorts; the failed Carrickfergus agreement signalled the end of Thurot.

The red flag featured on the French ceramic scene does have relevance to Thurot; it does not feature in, nor would it have any apparent relevance to the Italian scenes.

Taking into consideration these points together with the political climate, I suspect that the Sèvres artist made a clever, satirical use of the Tito pictures. And I favour Thurot as his subject.

Was Miriam Weston of Sound Mind?

◇◇◇

The Westons of Jane Austen's family are kinsmen of the Chancery case of *Weston con Weston and Weston*. (Properties establish a link through author Jane Austen's great, great aunt, Jane Austen who married into the Stringer family; who married into the Westons. Figure 1.) Figure 2 shows the family tree of the key protagonists.

The cause of Chancery was a dispute over the will of Miriam Weston, dated 11th December 1848 and, in particular, the codicils dated the same day and a further one added on 17th January 1849.

The Will extends to six large pages but the extracts given below give the gist of the content relevant to Chancery.

> *This is the last Will and Testament of me Miriam Weston of North End Terrace, Fulham, Middlesex, widow ... my executrixes and trustees ... shall purchase of the trustees of the Family Settlement ... in the year*

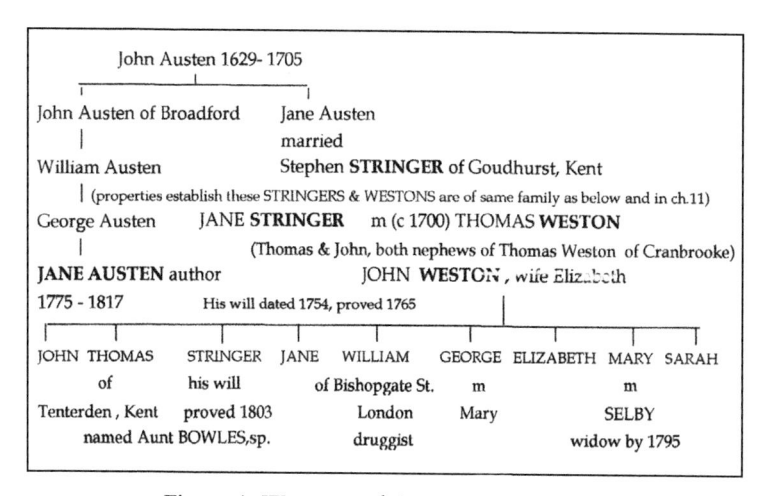

```
                John Austen 1629-1705
                         |
         _____
         |                         |
John Austen of Broadford     Jane Austen
         |                    married
William Austen              Stephen STRINGER of Goudhurst, Kent
         | (properties establish these STRINGERS & WESTONS are of same family as below and in ch.11)
George Austen      JANE STRINGER    m (c 1700) THOMAS WESTON
         |                    (Thomas & John, both nephews of Thomas Weston of Cranbrooke)
JANE AUSTEN author                JOHN WESTON, wife Elizabeth
1775 - 1817       His will dated 1754, proved 1765
                                    |
   _____
   |        |         |         |         |        |        |
JOHN     THOMAS   STRINGER   JANE    WILLIAM   GEORGE  ELIZABETH  MARY  SARAH
  of                 his will        of Bishopgate St.    m                 m
Tenterden, Kent    proved 1803        London          Mary              SELBY
named Aunt BOWLES,sp.                druggist                       widow by 1795
```

Figure 1. Weston and Austen Connections

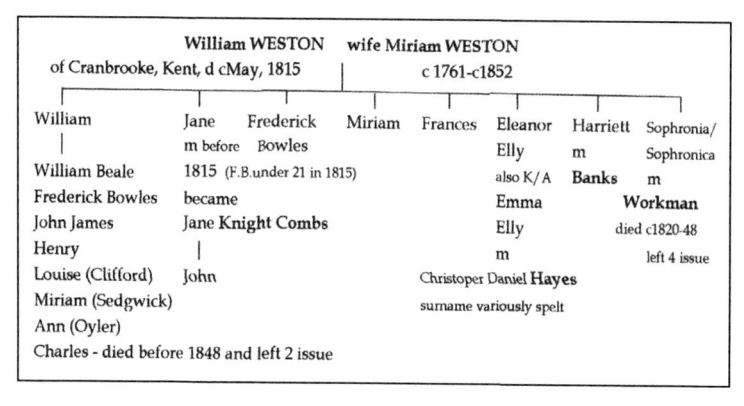

```
              William WESTON        wife Miriam WESTON
     of Cranbrooke, Kent, d cMay, 1815  |   c 1761-c1852
                                    |
  _____
  |       |                |        |        |         |         |
William  Jane   Frederick  Miriam  Frances  Eleanor  Harriett  Sophronia/
  |     m before  Bowles                    Elly       m       Sophronica
William Beale   1815 (F.B.under 21 in 1815)  also K/A  Banks     m
Frederick Bowles  became                      Emma            Workman
John James      Jane Knight Combs             Elly           died c1820-48
Henry              |                           m              left 4 issue
Louise (Clifford)  John              Christoper Daniel Hayes
Miriam (Sedgwick)                    surname variously spelt
Ann (Oyler)
Charles - died before 1848 and left 2 issue
```

Figure 2. Miriam Weston's family

Figures 1 and 2 are taken from *Billingsley, Brampton and Beyond: In search of The Weston Connection*

one thousand eight hundred and twenty, six cottages ... near Cranbrook in the County of Kent in the same settlement mentioned for as much money as they are fairly worth and ... convey the said cottages unto my granddaughters Louisa Clifford Miriam Sedgwick and Ann Oyler and their heirs ...

I direct ... to pay such a sum of money as should be equal to what a farm called Beach Farm also ... in the said settlement together with the timber thereon and all appurtenant thereunto shall be sold ... one fifth unto each of my grandchildren William Beal Weston Frederick Bowles Weston John James Weston Henry Weston and one fifth to the two children of my late grandson Charles Weston ... if any of my said grandsons shall die ... children alive ... shall take among them the one fifth share their father would have taken ... And I request ... trustees ... give my grandson William Beale Weston the first option of purchasing the said farm ... at a fair valuation ...

And inasmuch as by the said Settlement the sum of one thousand pounds ... to be set apart in trust for my daughter Jane Knight Combs and her children and the residue of the monies ... settled upon my other five daughters Sophronia (since deceased) Miriam Harriett Frances and Eleanor Elly and their children in equal shares ... but (if it does) *not turn out to be equal to one thousand pounds apiece I direct my executrixes in such a case to advance out of my estate sufficient money to make up the shares ...*

And as to all the Rest and Residue of my estate ... I give ... upon the trusts ... namely one sixth part thereof to divide and pay the same amongst the four children of my deceased daughter Sophronia Workman ... to pay one other equal sixth part unto my daughter Miriam ... and one other ... unto my daughter Frances ...

And upon further trust to invest the remaining three sixth parts on Government or real securities or

Parliamentary Funds of Great Britain ... as to one of the three ... to pay the dividends ... into the proper hands of my daughter Jane Knight Combs ... as to one of the other said three ... to pay the dividends ... into the proper hands of my daughter Harriot Banks ...as to the remaining share to permit my said daughter Emma Elly wife of Christopher Daniel Hayes ... the same ...

... if any person or persons benefitted by this my Will shall institute any suit at Law or in Equity or raise any dispute or demand whatsoever concerning the estate of my late husband ... or ... execution of this Will or ... concerning the non-performance or non execution of the trusts ... or concerning any sum or sums of money which have been or ought to have been received ... then the benefit or share and interest under this my will of such person or persons shall be forfeited ... and if either of my sons in law shall so offend it shall be taken to be the act of his wife and children ...

And I appoint my daughters Miriam Weston and Frances Weston executrixes and trustees of this my will and I hereby revoke all former wills by me at any time made In witness whereof I have ... set my hand this eleventh day of December in the year of our Lord one thousand eight hundred and forty eight – (signed M Weston) *... in the presence of us present at the same time ... our names as witnesses* (signed Sophia Brown servant to Mrs Weston – Henry Topp Clerk to Messes Scott & Combs St Mildred Court London

Whereas I have since making my will had reason to alter my mind concerning my grandsons John James Weston and Henry Weston Now I do hereby revoke the bequest to them of one fifth apiece of the sum at which the Beach Farm shall be sold for and

direct that the said two fifths shall fall into the residue of my estate and be held by my executrixes upon the trusts in my will ... Witness my hand this eleventh day of December one thousand eight hundred and forty eight – (signed M Weston) *Signed by the testatrise as a Codicil to her Will in the presence of us present at the same time ...* (signed Sophia Brown – Henry Topp)

I Miriam Weston to give to my daughters Miriam and Frances all the household furniture with the linen and plate belonging to me – (signed Miriam Weston) *... subscribed our names as witnesses* (signed Miriam Weston – Jane ?Butler/Buller – Sophia Brown Servant to Mrs Weston) *17 Jany 1849*

In the Prerogative Court of Canterbury
In the Goods of Miriam Weston Widow deceased
    Appeared Personally Jane ?Butler/Buller of No 1 North End Terrace ... Spinster ... one of the subscribed witnesses to the second and last Codicil to the last will ... of Miriam Weston formerly of Edward Square Kensington but late of North End Terrace ... further made oath that the said words name and date were so written at the end of the said codicil by Frances Weston Spinster the daughter of the deceased ... (signed Jane ?Butler/Buller) – *On the seventeenth day of May one thousand eight hundred and fifty two ...*
    Proved at London with two codicils 20th May 1852 ... by the oaths of Miriam Weston and Frances Weston ...

It will come as no surprise to the reader that 'Mr John Weston', in a conversation with Sophia Brown recorded in Chancery, *expressed that he had been cut out of Mrs Weston's will very improperly he thought.*

But before the story, revealed through the affidavits of witnesses, begins proper, a little more information can be added to that provided by Miriam in her will.

We learn from **the will of William Weston of Cranbrooke, dated 3rd March 1815** (proved May 1815 after his death), that, in addition to the six daughters also mentioned in the later will of Miriam, he had a son William Weston and son Frederick Bowles Weston.

Seemingly, Jane was the only daughter married at the time. The fact that William appoints Peter Wm Smith (of Reading,

Figure 3. 'The Momentous Interview' by H.K. Browne

Berkshire) and Thomas Weston guardians for his children "at the death of his wife", suggests some were of a young age. Certainly Frederick was under twenty-one.

Son William was left only fifty pounds. The will followed on with

> "... *the reason why I do not give him greater benefit under this Will is because I consider him already provided for ...*"

In his will, William refers to his dear wife (and sole executrix) as Marian and to one of his daughters as Marianne. However,

Figure 4. 'In Conference' by H.K. Browne

in the codicil (dated 11th March 1815), in which he gives his sole executrix the full power to sell and dispose of any of his estates, except the old Mansion house left to Frederick Bowles Weston, the executrix is referred to as Miriam. And Miriam subsequently refers to a daughter as Miriam, with no mention of a Marianne. This rather loose use of names is by no means unusual but of no help to research.

The question of whether Miriam Weston was of sound mind when she wrote her will and codicils is one which is raised in the eighty-three pages of a bound volume of depositions of 1852 (statements taken mostly in July). I have noted key factors from which to build the picture.

Figure 5. 'Bearer of Evil Tidings' by H.K. Browne

An account of circumstances surrounding the will is given, in varying lengths, by Henry Topp, clerk at the firm of Scott and Combs, of which Miriam Weston's grandson John Comb/s is a principal; John Combs himself; Sophia Brown, servant to the same Miriam Weston and Jane Butler/Buller, an acquaintance of long standing and more recently also a neighbour of Miriam's.

Henry Topp witnessed the signing of the will and first codicil.

This took place at Mrs Weston's home, near the Hammersmith Gate at Fulham, where, he states, he was let into the house by Miss Frances Weston.

He recalls that Mrs Weston made a remark respecting two of her grandsons William James and Henry ... *they shall have none of my money – they have offended me.*

Henry later signs another statement correcting the names; he says he made a mistake and that she said 'John James'.

Although he is aware that Mr Combs has an interest in the will in question through his mother, Henry confirms that he is not himself related or indebted.

The reliability of Henry Topp's statement is put in some doubt; firstly by the critical wrong naming of a grandson who was eventually excluded from the will; secondly, there are some points on which his statement does not agree with that made by Sophia Brown, though in this respect we have to judge which of them is more likely to be correct.

Sophia states that Miss Frances Weston was away from home on the day of the will signing. Frances could not, therefore have let Henry into the house.

Henry claims that Mrs Weston was present when the first codicil was written, Sophia says otherwise.

Sophia Brown was the only person to witness all three documents – the will plus two codicils. She left the employ of Mrs Weston in February 1849 after four and a half years in her service. It was Sophia who ascribed an age (90, or near 90) to Mrs Weston at the time of her death. In her statement she tells us that

> *When Miss Weston* (Miriam) *had told me beforehand that I was to sign a paper or 'the will' I told her I would rather have nothing to do with it ... for I thought it not unlikely that it might lead to some disputes for she and her mother was so given to disagree ... there was such frequent wrangling between her and her mother.*

Sophia recalled that when Mrs M Weston had said she "*wanted some little alteration*" Mr Combs told her it was too late unless she had a fresh will made and she sayed "*never Mind*".

In answer to the question of the state of mind of Mrs Weston, Sophia *cannot say ...* (she was) ... *in her right mind. I refer to her not letting her daughter have but hardly any fire when I was cooking ... she was quiet enough the day the will was signed.*

She later comes back to this topic. *I cannot say that Mrs Weston was not of sound mind (as much at least as she ever was).*

It was, of course, when Sophia was with a new master that she was called upon to make a statement. Evidently she had made one statement prior to the extracts quoted above, as she goes on to describe the first approach. Her new master (not named) had directed her to accompany Mr Combs to the office of Mr Denne and Mr Jellicoe.

Later Miss Frances Weston and her sister Mrs Hays had called and told her they had heard of her visit to ?Deveton Commons and commented that they should have been obliged if Sophia had let them know. One of them had remarked that they *should be left without a shilling.*

Sophia stated she had told them (it is not clear whether "them" refers to Denne and Jellicoe or Frances and her sister) that she *considered that Miss Weston had influence over her mother at different times – though I did not know that she influenced her about the will*. She had gone to the office of Denne and Jellicoe with her sister (who, incidentally, had been with Mrs Miriam Weston for eleven years prior to Sophia taking up the position) and reports *Mr Combes sayed my expenses would be paid and Mr Denne … gave my sister and me half a sovereign each – though we neither of us wished for anything of the kind*.

Sophia reiterates the claim that Mrs Miriam Weston was, particularly as she got older, much under the influence of Misses Frances and Miriam, especially Miriam. And later states … *Miriam Weston would get over the deceased in almost anything by a little management*. It was this daughter who had offered Sophia *a glup of wine* as she had felt nervous about signing the will, but she had declined.

At this point, Sophia was quick to stress her superior moral fibre by noting that Tealy, a servant who lived next door, had had a *Glup of wine – or gin* when she had to sign something and was nervous.

Jane Butler/Buller, a 55-year-old spinster and neighbor of Mrs Weston's for the past 18-20 years, first met the deceased and her daughters when they were living in Edward's Square. She witnessed only the second codicil and, therefore, has little to add of importance to the content of the will and first codicil; save two questions regarding the general propriety of the drawing up of the documents. Jane notes that Mrs Weston signed without wearing her spectacles and questions when some of the content may have been written; she recalls something being said about putting in the date later and Mrs Weston saying *Yes do my dear.*

It is interesting that Miriam did not wear her spectacles when signing the second codicil. We do not know the time of day of that signing but, according to John Combs (aged 35 in 1852), the will itself was read by daylight and signed by candlelight – about four o'clock.

John Combs's comments support Sophia Brown's observation that Mrs Weston was under the influence of her daughter Miriam, but says that it was on domestic, unimportant things.

The will of 1848 was not the first to have been drawn up for Miriam by her grandson. He had acted for her since 1840, when he prepared her will and a codicil to that will in 1842. In 1848, Miriam his aunt, had come to his office in St. Mildred's Court and said Mrs Miriam Weston had determined the will should not stand and that she had torn it up (whether it had actually been torn up was later brought into question).

A reason given was that an executor, Reverend Peter French, had intimated he would not act. (Would a change of executor warrant a total rewriting of a will? Probably not.) Later we will come to claims of other reasons for changing the will.

Following the visit from his Aunt Miriam, John Combs and his clerk Henry Topp called to see Mrs Weston at her home. Combs cannot recollect whether or not it was by appointment.

He does recall, however, the need to send Topp to get a sheet of paper at Hammersmith – Combs had forgotten *one in which to envelope the will* – whilst he went on to his grandmother's home alone. He also confirms that on his arrival he found his mother (Mrs Weston's daughter, Jane Knight Combs) sitting with his grandmother and states that it was ...*quite a surprise to me finding my mother there.*

There were no statements to corroborate his version of the early part of the interview but he relayed the following outcomes, as he remembered them.

The general scheme of her instructions was in the first instance to get rid as it were of her grandchildren, the children of her late son William. (The will refers only to daughter Sophronia and grandson Charles as having died. In view of the will of William's father in 1815, William would not be expected to feature in this will whether still living or not, so this reference cannot be accepted as a full confirmation of his death.) ... *and divide it* (the property and money) *between her daughters and their children ... no doubt I asked her 'Now Miriam, what will you do first and what will you do next ... and what will you do with the rest of your property' and so on ... I recollect that when she mentioned the cottages I did not feel sure, knowing that my father had bought several cottages ... on settlement ...*

Combs said he asked Frances to produce the original will. There was no claim at this stage that it had, in fact, been torn up.

The statement of John Combs goes on to say he *was aware from communications with my grandmother that she was disposed to think that her former will was too stringent ... especially as regarded her other unmarried daughter Miss Frances Weston ... 'I think Frances should have her money as well as Miriam'* ...

On 1.12.1848 he had *had tea with my grandmother and two aunts* and had taken notes for the new will. He then itemizes bequests – in essence much the same as appear in Miriam's will – but four of the lines have been altered; they are confused and the sequence of those lines is hard to decipher. Those lines follow on in his statement with *Her directions were, as it had been in her previous will I think ... I noted down from her dictation the names of her said grandchildren ... a few observations passed between us as to one of her grandsons Charles being dead, and his share going to his two children* (he later says that he does not know the names of these, the two children of Charles Weston, deceased son of William Weston). He confirms here that the indication that the earlier will had been destroyed had been a mistake and *it turned out to be the codicil.*

More details as to the distribution of the estates are given and then an explanation of *the clause 'as to going to law' ... cutting off any of her family who should file a bill or otherwise take any legal steps in reference to the settlement* was because this line of action was *supposed to have been contemplated by some Branch of the family.*

John Combs's version of his grandmother saying, on the eleventh of December, 1848 *John and Henry will have none of my property ...* was similar to that of Henry Topp's. He did not know from his grandmother why she had cut out her grandsons but said *I conjectured in my own mind what was the cause.*

Unfortunately, he does not expand on this. What was said next by him differs from Sophia Brown's account. According to Combs he said that it *would need a codicil* and denies saying that it was too late and would need another will.

In addition to his affidavit, there was included as evidence, a letter written by Combs to his grandmother after a visit, though precisely to what he refers and when the course of action he refers to was decided upon, is not clear. ... *This course appears to me in a legal and practical point of view much preferable to the other course ... some of them being abroad and one dead leaving infant children ... other course would necessarily lead to trouble and expense and the incurring of responsibility in taking security ...*

He insists in his statement that he acted scrupulously. He was paid five sovereigns for his work in drawing up the will. As to how much he benefitted from the revisions, John Combs states *The deceased's personal estate is I believe of the value of somewhere about £22,000 – but I have no knowledge on the point.* And he concludes that the new will/codicil will make a difference of about £15 to him.

I have not found the judgement of this dispute.

Introduction to Group III

◇◇◇

One of my sons made me a birthday present of the book *Mauve* by Simon Garfield. He gave the reason for his choice as my quoting (or misquoting) from Jenny Fisher's lovely poem *Warning* – my excuse for errant behaviour. The poem begins

> *When I am an old woman I shall wear purple*
> *With a red hat which doesn't go, and doesn't suit me.*
> *And I shall spend my pension on brandy …*

(My other son bought me a bottle of Bacardi Ginger – because of my love of ginger, obviously.)

It transpired that *Mauve* had a lot of unexpected meaning for me. The book describes the discovery, by William Perkin, of the world's first synthetic dye in 1856, and the subsequent significance for industry in textiles, foods and medicines. Elements in *Mauve* were reminiscent of an essay I had written in April 1985 – on a particular synthetic dye – submitted towards a BSc in Dietetics.

At that time, I was a mature student with a family. One of my children had asthma attacks (he disliked being referred to as an asthmatic; in his words, aged 10 years, "I'm not an asthmatic, most of the time I am okay"). There were some scary moments, not least before the time came when he was fully aware of when, and what action to take if in difficulty when out with friends.

This could have had a bearing on why I chose to look specifically at the use of the (red) synthetic dye, ponceau 4R, in food and implication in allergy. Professionally, it was of interest because of a sister compound, an orange dye called tartrazine, which was being studied in relation to attention deficit and other learning and behavioural disorders.

In more recent times, concern about the promotion of sweeteners, in particular to children, and in particular sweeteners (and derivatives of sweeteners) that use isolated phenylalanine, finally led me to write another essay.

The focus of that essay is less on *why* it is a bad policy and more on *how* it is possible to implement a public health policy that is clearly wrong. It questions whether the drive for the policy is largely political, commercial, or a partnership of vested interests that are being put before the public interest.

Both of these essays are now reproduced in this book.

Since writing the latter essay, the Government's policy has become further entrenched.

A revision has been made to the UK's Nutrient Profiling Model (NPM) of 2004/5. Essentially, the NPM provides a scoring system for placing products into healthy or unhealthy categories. This in turn may inform such things as food marketing and labelling.

The main change to the NPM (from a description of 'total sugars' to 'free sugars') was *deemed necessary* because *the NPM 2004/5 score does not reflect considerations such as encouraging artificially sweetened beverages.*

In spite of this being the reason a modification was "deemed necessary", the quoted phrase that followed is the only direct reference to sweeteners, and this in an appendix, not the main body of the document – in appendix D in relation to the differing French approach.

The procedure towards the acceptance of the draft 2018 NPM was perfunctory, comprising a set of structured questions for reviewers to answer.

However, official reviewers of the modified NPM circumvented the structured questions presented to them, in order to raise their concerns. They queried why the recommendations of the World Health Organisation (WHO) were ignored and ratings using food groups and variety not considered. And queried why the NPM ratings had not been compared with the views of nutrition professionals.

The reviewer's concerns were not properly addressed but dismissed on the grounds that their *terms of reference did not include validation of the draft 2018 NPM (modified)*.

As a consequence – and clearly the whole purpose of the manoevre – diet drinks score highly (as healthy) whilst pure fruit juices score poorly (as unhealthy, and advice given that intake should be no more than 150mls per day). A shameful outcome that perpetuates misleading public health information.

I have no 'terms of reference' that I have to abide by: I can, and will say that the combination of (i) a policy that promotes the use of sweeteners and (ii) an undisclosed –though legal – use of isolated phenylalanine (as in neotame and advantame) is abhorrent. It denies choice and further renders the figures of Acceptable Daily Intake (ADI) meaningless (already so because, on current knowledge, there are no tests that can establish safety – especially important for children).

Unfortunately, being an old woman is double edged: a freedom to speak out, but no one listens.

PONCEAU 4R – ITS USE IN FOOD AND IMPLICATION IN ALLERGY

◇◇◇

BY P. GARDNER

Essay submitted as an assessment
Towards BSc in dietetics
Leeds Polytechnic

APRIL 1985

The acceptance of a food depends initially upon its appearance. It needs to look attractive and a major contributing factor to this is the colour. In fact, food colour accounts for forty-five per cent of the total quality scale (Kramer and Twigg, 1956 cited by Eskin).

Natural colour pigments found in foods are subject to chemical changes which result in alterations in or loss of colour. It will be appreciated that the various conditions involved in the processing of food may often promote these undesirable changes. Even though taste, texture and nutritional content may not be affected the product will, nevertheless, be unacceptable without the restoration of the food's natural colour. The addition of colour may also be required to make new, insipid products attractive or to standardize foods which vary in colour.

The choice of food colours now available to manufacturers includes synthetic as well as natural colours. All colour, whether synthesized or natural, depends upon a chemical structure that is a conjugated system of double bonds alternating with a single bond, giving an arrangement of electrons sensitive to the incident of light. The synthetic colours with a chemical structure that is not found in natural pigments have been grouped according to their particular chemical structure, there being five groups of dyes; azo, triarylmethane, xanthene, quinolone and indigoid.

Ponceau 4R, a red colouring agent, belongs to the azo group. The azo dyes, which contain a $-N=N-$ group, are the most widely used synthetic colours. Nitrogen in the molecule intensifies the colour and consequently only a minute amount is needed to give a good depth of colour. This, together with the ease of their production, the consistency, stability and range and brilliance of shade, is the reason for their popularity with food manufacturers.

It should be pointed out that although azo dyes are widely used, caramel, a non-synthetic agent, still accounts for 98% of all colouring matter. The low percentage value for the widely used alternative dyes is partly explained by their having a high tinctorial strength.

Before a colouring agent can be permitted for use in any food it must be shown to be harmless to the health of the consumer. In order to establish this, short-term and long-term toxicity trials are carried out on animals. The trials test for mutagenicity, teratogenicity and carcinogenicity and use two animal species, one of which must be non-rodent.

The governing body responsible for approving food colours within the United Kingdom was, until recently, the Food Additives and Contaminants Committee (FACC) founded in 1964. It has now amalgamated with the Food Standards Committee to form the Food Advisory Committee (FAC).

In 1979 the then FACC gave an interim report on the 'Review of the Colouring Matter in the Food Regulations of 1973'. It listed food colours recommended for unconditional or conditional acceptance, using an acceptability grading system which, for food additives as a whole, comprised six grades (A–F). All the colours except one (Patent Blue V), fell into category A or B. Grade A colours are those which available evidence suggests may be used without qualification; grade B includes colours provisionally acceptable but requiring additional evidence of safety to be provided within five years.

Ponceau 4R was placed in category B.

It is interesting to note that, although Ponceau 4R was included in the permitted list in the 'Colouring Matter in Food Regulations, 1957', it was 22 years later before further toxicological data was requested.

A representative of the Food Additives Branch of the Ministry of Agriculture, Fisheries and Food stated in a personal communication that *these data have since been received and evaluated by the Committee on Toxicology (COT) which has subsequently classified ponceau 4R as acceptable for use in food, group A.*

The FAC is now receiving data collected as a result of the earlier report and its final report, which will include the report of the COT, and its recommendations, will be published for public comment once the review is complete.

Once a colour is permitted there is no restriction imposed on the level at which it can be added, although there are some foods from which added colour is prohibited, namely raw or unprocessed meat, game, poultry, fish, fruit, vegetables, tea, coffee, coffee products, condensed or dried milk.

In 1976 a working party was set up to obtain information on dietary intake of food colours, the results of which are given in the 1979 FACC interim report previously referred to.

There are obviously going to be many individual variations in the range and quantity of foods eaten and not all similar commodities, e.g. ice cream, will contain the same level of colour. To take into account some of these variations intakes of different 'types' of diet were estimated.

The average diet comprised a cross section of foods with an average intake of coloured foods. It was then sub-divided to allow for people who either had a preference for one particular colour or who consumed the products containing the maximum level of added colour.

Full details of estimated intakes of colours are given in appendix II and of ponceau 4R specifically in appendices III to VI but a summary is as follows:

Type of Diet	mg/day of ponceau 4R
Adult average diet with a cross section of coloured foods containing average levels of colour	.88
Average quantity of coloured foods, average levels of colour, but with a bias for ponceau 4R	4.3
(NB if the foods contained maximum levels of colour)	(25.8)
Average quantity, cross section of coloured foods (no bias) but maximum levels of colour	3.47
Higher than average quantity of coloured foods, but a cross-section and average levels	1.72
Child (25kg) average, cross section of coloured foods containing average levels of colour	1.03
(bias for ponceau 4R at average levels of colour)	(6.3)

It was thought to be beyond the realms of likelihood that someone would have an 'extreme' diet which also contained the maximum levels of colour so it was concluded that consumption was well within safe limits. However, considering how large is the difference between the average and maximum levels of ponceau 4R used (4.3mg cf 25.8mg), it seems feasible that some people may have exceeded the then Acceptable Daily Intake (ADI) quoted as 0.15 mg/kg body weight (that is 10.5mg for a 70kg man and 3.75 for a 25kg child).

Here it should be mentioned that the European Commission's Scientific Committee for Food have since established for ponceau 4R an ADI of 0.4mg/kg body weight (MAFF 1985) following the toxicity trials.

It has been recommended that no colour should be added to infant foods (MAFF, 1979). Although there is no regulation to this effect, manufacturers do follow the recommendation. It seems ironic, therefore, that some foods aimed particularly at children, for example the 'Mr Men' yoghurts, are then made pronouncedly more colourful than similar products aimed more widely.

Children do tend to be attracted to colourful and sweet foods so to allow for this the 'child's diet' has the adult intake of certain commodities multiplied by 1.5. Such commodities which contain ponceau 4R are dessert mixes, flour confectionary, jellies and preserves. Although this one adjustment has been made to the quantities eaten, it will be noted that the level of colouring is taken as average and as already pointed out some products may be more highly coloured for children.

Given the need for some use of colouring agents and the advantages of azo dyes why be concerned with the extent of the use of ponceau 4R?

Lockey (1959, cited by MacGibbon) first noted an adverse reaction to another dye, tartrazine, when a patient receiving a tartrazine-containing steroid therapy developed urticaria. Since then there has been increasing concern that some azo dyes, including ponceau 4R, elicit allergic responses in susceptible people.

It is not possible on the evidence available to give accurate details of the incidence of allergy to ponceau 4R. Two basic problems confront the investigator; firstly to establish that symptoms observed are caused by the dye and secondly to determine whether or not the reaction is an allergic response.

Adverse reactions to ponceau 4R may not be recognized as such because of its widespread use in a variety of foods. In fact a reaction may become associated with the main ingredient of the food rather than the additive (Freedman, 1977a).

If a reaction to ponceau 4R, or to azo dyes in general, is suspected the method most generally used for confirming the diagnosis is by elimination and challenge. Any foods (or drugs, cosmetics or toothpastes) which contain azo dyes are eliminated from the diet until the symptoms subside. The patient is then challenged with the dye and any symptoms observed. Most studies on azo dyes relate to tartrazine, but one study reported that 15% of patients with chronic urticaria showed sensitivity to ponceau 4R (Mikkelson, Larsen and Tarding, 1978). However, this cannot be extrapolated meaningfully, by using the percentage of people in the population with urticaria, to determine the percentage of the population sensitive to ponceau 4R. To do this would be to assume that the patients with urticaria have no greater tendency to a sensitivity to ponceau 4R than normal subjects.

Even when an adverse reaction has been attributed to ponceau 4R there can be difficulty in defining that it is an allergic response because there are three other types of reaction to food which may resemble an allergy; 1) food idiosyncrasies, which may be due to inborn errors, 2) intoxication and 3) pseudo-allergic reactions, caused by histamine or plant lectins – capable of activating T-lymphocytes non-specifically (Bleumink, 1983).

These various types of reaction all come under the general heading of food intolerance. Only an immunological response can be classed as a true allergy. Immunological responses can be divided into four main types but it should be noted that in any particular disease process more than one mechanism may operate.

Type 1 represents the immediate hypersensitivity reaction initiated between the allergen or antigen and its specific immunoglobulin type E (IgE) or short-term IgG antibody on the surface of mast cells. This results in the release of pre-formed vasoactive substances, such as histamine and the synthesis of others, such as prostaglandins.

Type II is the cytotoxic reaction. It usually involves antibodies of the IgG or IgM immunoglobulin class. The antigen with which the antibody reacts may be part of the cell surface structure or an exogenous antigen absorbed to the cell surface. The activation of an enzyme system of serum proteins called complement may occur, leading to cell lysis and tissue damage.

Type III is an antigen-antibody complex reaction. The antigen combines with an IgM or IgG class antibody, generally in the presence of antigen excess, with the formation of immune complexes. Complement is activated. The immune complexes are deposited in the vessel walls and tissue damage occurs.

Type IV is also known as delayed hypersensitivity or cell mediated reaction. It is not associated with any demonstrable circulating antibody but is known to involve sensitized T-lymphocytes, which react with the antigen. The lymphocytes release a variety of reactive substances called lymphokines, which cause infiltration of the site by lymphocytes and macrophages.

An immunological response can manifest itself in numerous ways, such as anaphylaxis, urticaria, eczema, rhinitis, asthma, contact dermatitis and oedema.

Azo dyes have been implicated among the possible causes of some of these symptoms; urticaria (Lockey, 1959, Michaëlsson and Juhlin, 1973); asthma (Rosenhall and Zetterström, 1973,

Stenius et al, 1976); rhinitis (Michaëlsson and Juhlin, 1973); contact dermatitis (Kgzakat, Tashiro and Sano, 1980) and angio-oedema (Michaëlsson and Juhlin, 1973), which suggests an allergic reaction is possibly involved.

Ponceau 4R is, like other food additives, of too low a molecular weight to act as an antigen, which are usually glycolproteins with a molecular weight of 20–40,000 (Walter-smith, 1978). Therefore, if it does cause an allergic reaction it must be acting as an hapten, combining with a body or dietary protein which then makes it capable of eliciting an allergic response.

This was the approach taken by Justin-Davies in 1984. The immunological potential of ponceau 4R was studied, using a milk protein B lactoglobulin as the protein conjugate, but it was not conclusive that the dye did increase the antigenic potential of the protein.

There is contradictory opinion as to which type of immune response is implicated in food allergic disease. Zanussi (1978) and Denman (1980) suggest type 1 is the most likely, partly because of the often rapid reaction to the antigen. Elevated serum IgE levels indicate a type 1 hypersensitivity and this has been found in 30% of patients with food allergic disease. However, these patients do not necessarily react to azo dyes and also, as they may be hypersensitive to additional allergens, such as house dust, further tests would be necessary to determine the specificity of the IgE's. This can be done with radio allergosorbent tests (RAST) which have been found to have good correlation with provocation methods and skin testing.

Bleumink (1983), also supports the view that evidence suggests a type 1 response but also may involve a type III response. Several cases have been reported of elevated circulating IgG and evidence of complement consumption; namely a decrease in plasma C3 in some patients with urticaria and angio-oedema (Sissons, Peters, Gwyn-Williams and Boulton-Jones, 1974), though it is possible that the lower C3 level is a result of an intrinsic abnormality of the complement system itself rather than stress on the system.

According to Zanussi (1978) type III reaction is exceptional in response to food additives and MacGibbon (1983), concludes there is insufficient evidence that type I is responsible.

Another suggestion by Bleumink (1983) is that a person may become sensitized by a low molecular weight substance becoming antigenic with a skin protein, causing a type IV reaction and resulting in contact dermatitis. Subsequent oral consumption of the same molecular weight agent may also then elicit a type IV allergic reaction. As ponceau 4R is used as a dye in cloth and cosmetics as well as in food this is a possibility to be considered.

Although azo dyes have been indicted as sensitizers more often than other food dyes they in fact exhibit the least binding ability of all the dyes (Michaëlsson and Jahlin, 1973), so it may be that the reaction is unrelated to haptens.

An alternative explanation is that the dye is exerting a pharmacological effect on the mast cell membrane, causing degranulation through a process other than an antigen-antibody reaction. The subsequent release of vaso active mediators could then produce the same symptoms as when released via an allergic reaction; consequently it is not possible to distinguish an allergic reaction from all other adverse reactions by the symptoms produced.

Cross reactivity has been noted between aspirin and tartrazine (Stenius, 1976) and aspirin has been shown to inhibit prostaglandin (PG) synthesis (Vane 1971), cited by Freedman). It has been suggested that in aspirin sensitive asthmatics a selective inhibition of PGE's (bronchodilators) could lead to unopposed broncho constriction by PGF's (Settipane, Chaffee and Klein,

1974 and Vane 1975). According to Zetterström (1972) (cited by Stenius) the effect of acetylsalicylic acid may be dose related, small doses inhibiting the dilating prostaglandins and larger doses inhibiting all prostaglandins with either no effect overall or a dilatation effect. Denman (1980) also notes that the degree of reactivity may be greatly influenced by immediate previous exposure of a reactive substance and over exposure may result in a masking of reactivity.

A worrying implication is that some patients may never have a frank attack of asthma after consumption of azo dyes but may have moderate but constant bronchial obstruction which is only partly controlled by medication (Stenius 1976).

As tartrazine has features in its chemical structure which are common to ponceau 4R it is possible that cross reactivity exists also with ponceau 4R and aspirin.

It may be questioned how relevant is the mechanism of the reaction when the test of most value in the diagnosis of sensitivity to ponceau 4R is still by elimination and challenge and the basic treatment one of elimination of the dye from the diet? Knowledge of the mechanism, however, would enable a prediction to be made as to the efficacy of the use of disodium cromoglycate, a drug sometimes used both as a diagnostic tool and also as an adjunct to conventional treatment.

Disodium cromoglycate (DSCG) stabilizes the mast cell membrane, inhibiting the release of vaso active mediators. If taken with, or prior to, a suspected allergen, it could prevent a type I allergic response from ensuing but would be of no use in a type IV reaction.

It was found by Freedman (1977) that DSCG did protect patients suffering from tartrazine induced asthma, when inhaled prior to challenge with tartrazine. However, prevention of an adverse reaction, although confirming the cause of the reaction, does not necessarily confirm an allergic reaction. It may be inhibiting the action of non-immunological stimuli (Orr and Cox, 1973), perhaps acting pharmacologically as aspirin.

It is apparent that there is much further work required in this field before mechanism is elucidated. The complexity of contributory factors, such as infection or fatigue, which can lead to variability in the occurrence of an allergic reaction, further complicates progress in diagnosis.

In spite of the unanswered questions there is little doubt that in some people ponceau 4R is involved in either causing or contributing to an adverse reaction whether or not it is of an immunological nature.

It is necessary, therefore, to know which foods and other commodities contain ponceau 4R so they can be avoided if required. Patients referred to a dietitian would of course be provided with information regarding current products, but as new products are constantly coming onto the market it would be more convenient and reassuring for the patient if this information was given on the labelled goods.

The Food Labelling Regulations, 1984, do not require that specific colours used are listed, only that the generic term, i.e. 'colour' is quoted. Although this may sometimes be followed by the named colour (ponceau 4R) EEC number (E124), or alternative name (Cochineal Red A). Perhaps it would be of more use if the label was required to state 'azo-colour' when applicable rather than simply 'colour'.

It is not required that medicines should be labelled with the colour content. A wise precaution would be to not prescribe azo coloured medicines for the treatment of any symptoms associated with an allergic reaction, even when a food related antigen is not suspected.

Furthermore, it is to be hoped that the increase in the ADI for ponceau 4R and its placing in category A from B will not encourage manufacturers to use the colour more indiscriminately as favourable toxicological tests bear no relation to the immunoreaginic potential of the dye, and an intense colour is not necessary.

Sometimes intensity of colour is associated with ripeness or freshness and this contributes to consumers' desirability for coloured foods. However, this desire is heightened through conditioning. A young child during a period of investigation and discovery is attracted to highly coloured objects. In order to direct the child's interest away from play and onto food the child's attention may be drawn to the colour of the food, for example "Look at this lovely red jelly", and thus associate pleasant food with intense colours.

If made aware of the lack of merit and possible disadvantages of artificially colouring foods, consumers could be conditioned to accept 'lightly' coloured processed foods as preferable to 'highly' coloured ones.

Reference

Bleumink E (1983) Pro.Nutr.Soc. 42 p219-231 'Immunological Aspects of Food Allergy'.

Denman A M (1980) Pro. of 'The First Food Allergy Workshop'. Chaired by Prof. R R A Coombs p49-52. Pub. Medical Education services Limited, Oxford 1980.

Freedman B J (1977a) Clinical Allergy Vol. 7 p417-421. 'A dietary free from additives in the management of allergic disease'.

Freedman B J (1977b) Clin. All. Vol. 7 p407-415. 'Asthma induced by sulphur dioxide, benzoate and tartrazine contained in orange drinks'.

Justin-Davies (1984) Project submitted at Leeds Polytechnic as an assessment towards BSc Dietetics 'A Study of the Immunological Potential of an azo dye – Ponceau 4R'.

Kgzakat, T, Tashiro M, Sano S (1980). Contact Dermatitis Aug. 6 (5)

330-336 'Pigmented contact dermatitis from azo dyes I. Cross-sensitivity in humans'.
Kramer A and Twigg B A (1956). Quality control for the canner and freezer, Canner Freezer 122, 16. Cited by N A M Eskin 'Plant pigments, Flavours and Textures'. Academic Press 1979.
Lockey S D (1959) Ann. Allergy 17:719 'Allergic reactions due to F D and C yellow No 5, tartrazine, an aniline dye used as a colouring and identifying agent in various steroids, cited by MacGibbon 1983.
MacGibbon B (1983) Pro. Nutr. Soc. 42 (2) 233-240. 'Adverse reactions to food additives'.
Michaëlsson and Juhlin (1973), Brit. J. of Derm. 88, 225 'Urticaria induced by preservatives and dye additives in food and drugs' cited by Stenius (1976).
Mikkelson H, Larsen J C, Tarding F (1978), Arch. Toxicol. Suppl. 1, 141, cited by MacGibbon.
Ministry of Agriculture, Fisheries and Food (1979). FACC Interim Report on the Review of the Colouring Matter in Food Regulations of 1973. Pub. London HMSO 1979.
Ministry of Agriculture, Fisheries and Food (1985), Food Additives Branch, personal communication.
Orr T S C and Cox J S G (1973). 8th International Congress of Allergology; Special sectional Meeting of Disodium Cromoglycate cited by Freedman 1977.
Rosenhall L and Zetterström O (1973) Läkartidningen, 70, 1417 'Asthma provoked by analgesics, food colourants and food preservatives', cited by Freedman (1977).
Settipane G A, Chafee F H and Klein D E (1974) J. of Allergy and Clinical Immunology, 53 200 'Aspirin intolerance II. A prospective study in an atopic and normal population', cited by Stenius (1976).
Sissons J G P, Peters D K, Gwyn Williams D, Bouton-Jones J M (1974). Lancet (2): 1350-1352, 'Skin lesions, angio-oedema and hpyocomplemtaemia'.
Stenius B S M and Lemola M (1976) Clin. All. 6, 119. 'Hypersensitivity to acetylsalicylic (ASA) and tartrazine in patients with asthma'.
Vane J R (1971) Nature: New Biology 23, 232 'Inhibition of prostaglandin synthesis as a mechanism of action for aspirin-like drugs', cited by Freedman (1977b).

Vane J R (1975) 'Allergy 74'. Proceedings of the 9th European Congress of Allergology and Clinical Immunology (Ed. M A Ganderton and A W Frankland) p79 Pitman Medical, cited by Freedman (1977b)

Walker-Smith J A (1978), Practitioner 220 (1318) 562-573, G I Allergy.

Zanussi C (1978) Chemical Toxicology as Food, 1st Ed. Elsevier/North Holland Biochemical Press. 'Allergic Potential of Food Additives'.

Zetterström O (1972) Analgetilcaintolerans. Astma atropi och, cited by Stenius (1976).

Appendices to Ponceau 4R

◇◇◇

Appendix I: Chemical Structure of Ponceau 4R

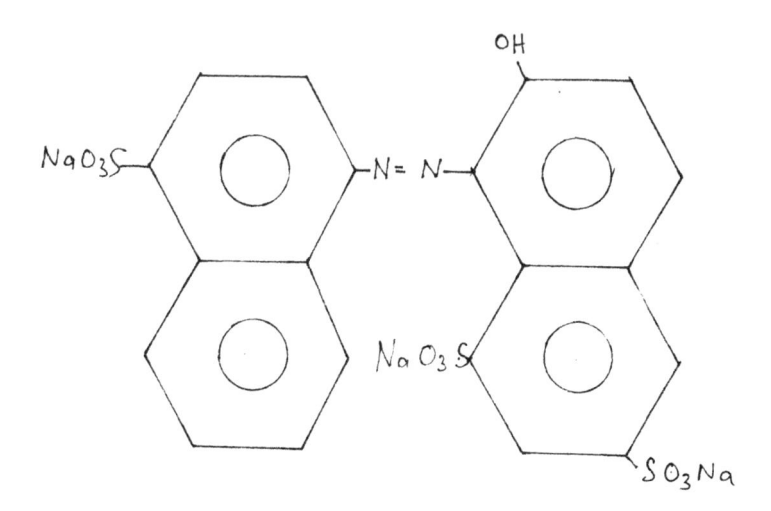

Appendix II. Summary Table of Intakes of Colours

Colour	ADI (mg/kg body-weight)	ADI (mg per 70 kg person)	Average Diet — Uncorrected daily intake of colour (average level of use) (mg)	Average Diet — Corrected daily intake of colour (maximum level of use) (mg)	Average Diet — Corrected daily intake of colour (average level of use) (mg)	Extreme Diet — ADI (mg per 70 kg person)	Extreme Diet — Corrected daily intake of colour (mg)	Child's Diet — ADI (mg per 25 kg child)	Child's Diet — Corrected daily intake of colour (mg)
1	2	3	4	5	6	7	8	9	10
Riboflavin E101	0·5*	35	1·25	0·01	0·01	35	0·02	12·5	0·02
Tartrazine E102	7·5	525	10·32	35·49	4·63	525	9·07	187·5	6·69
Quinoline Yellow E104	0·5	35	0·43	<0·005	<0·005	35	<0·005	12·5	<0·005
Yellow 2G	0·01	0·7	8·99	1·98	1·38	0·7	2·69	0·25	1·39
Sunset Yellow FCF E110	2·5	175	11·51	13·67	1·99	175	3·90	62·5	2·40
Orange G	0	0	8·62	0·03	0·02	0	0·03	0	0·02
Cochineal E120	*Restricted use*		5·26	0·69	0·48		0·94		0·61
Carmoisine E122	2·0	140	8·10	1·47	0·32	140	0·63	50	0·48
Amaranth E123	0·75	52·5	8·67	16·59	1·44	52·5	2·81	18·75	1·79
Ponceau 4R E124	0·15	10·5	4·30	3·47	0·88	10·5	1·72	3·75	1·03
Erythrosine BS E127	2·5	175	2·71	1·56	0·21	175	0·42	62·5	0·24
Red 2G	0·1	7	1·24	1·59	0·31	7	0·60	2·5	0·46
Solanthrene Blue RS E130†	0	0	0·72	<0·005	<0·005	0	<0·005	0	<0·005
Patent Blue V E131	2·5	175	0·03	<0·005	<0·005	175	<0·005	62·5	<0·005
Indigo Carmine E132	5·0	350	2·09	0·80	0·03	350	0·06	125	<0·005
Brilliant Blue FCF	2·5	175	0·50	<0·005	<0·005	175	<0·005	62·5	<0·005
Green S E142	5·0	350	1·46	0·19	0·08	350	0·16	125	0·08
Brown FK‡	0·05	3·5	3·16	0·23	0·21	3·5	0·42	1·25	0·32
Chocolate Brown FB	0	0	0·18	<0·005	<0·005	0	<0·005	0	<0·005
Chocolate Brown HT	2·5	175	41·51	13·35	9·76	175	19·15	62·5	14·62
Black PN E151	0·75	52·5	4·98	0·01	0·01	52·5	0·01	18·75	0·01
Black 7984 E152†	0	0	2·22	<0·005	<0·005	0	<0·005	0	<0·005
Carbon Black E153	*Restricted use*		2·10	0·83	0·09		0·18	0	0·21
β-Carotene E160(a)	5·0**	350	6·08	5·24	0·23	350	0·45	125	0·23
Annatto E160(b)	1·5	105	1·28	2·82	1·19	105	2·32	37·5	1·19
Canthaxanthin E161(g)	25·0	1750	0·005	0·005	<0·005	1750	<0·005	625	<0·005
Titanium dioxide E171	*Restricted use*		20·31	34·93	8·01		15·71		14·17
Iron oxides and hydroxides E172	No limit	No limit	0·12	0·18	0·11	No limit	0·21	No limit	0·11

*ADI recommended by the Joint FAO/WHO Expert Committee on Food Additives.

†The sale of food containing these colours will not be permitted in the UK after 1 January 1978.

‡The intake of Brown FK from kippers is not included in the Table. Manufacturers' figures suggest that an 'average' consumer will consume approximately 200g of kippers per month, although many consumers may eat this amount in a week. The average level of Brown FK in kippers is approximately 2·4 mg/100g of product, so that the intake of Brown FK from this source would be approximately 0·16 mg/day for our imagined 'average' consumer and approximately 0·69 mg/day for the consumer eating 200g of kippers per week. Clearly these intake levels have to be borne in mind when the intakes of Brown FK from the three diets are considered.

**Sum of the carotenoids beta-carotene, beta-apo-8'-carotenal (C30) and ethyl ester of beta-apo-8'-carotenoic acid (C30).

Intakes exceeding the ADI are italicised. Colours at present permitted by UK Regulations for general use in food and considered by the SCF but not included in the Table are (excluding caramel): curcumin, Fast Yellow AB, orchil, chlorophyll, copper complexes of chlorophyll and chlorophyllin, alpha- and gamma-carotenes, lycopene, beta-apo-8'-carotenal (C30), ethyl ester of beta-apo-8'-carotenoic acid (C30), other permitted xanthophylls (other than cantaxanthin), Beetroot Red and anthocyanins. Colours permitted for certain purposes only and considered by the SCF but not included in the Table are aluminium, silver, gold, Pigment Rubine and Burnt Umber. (The sale of food containing Fast Yellow AB, orchil and Burnt Umber will not be permitted in the UK after 1 January 1978).

Appendix III. Average diet/average level of use

Colour: PONCEAU 4R E124

Food 1	Intake of food (g/day) 2	Level of colour in food (mg/kg) 3	Uncorrected intake of colour from food (mg/day; $\frac{\text{Col 2} \times \text{Col 3}}{1000}$) 4	Corrected intake of colour from food (mg/day) 5
Breakfast cereals	12·4			
Butter and margarine	37·2			
Canned fruit	15·2	82·3	1·25	0·62
Canned soup	12·1	1·5	0·02	<0·005
Canned vegetables	31·8			
Cheese	15·3			
Chocolate and sugar confectionery	16·1	55·0	0·89	0·03
Dessert mixes	7·9	3·1	0·02	<0·005
Dry mixes (other than dessert mixes)	5·8	13·9	0·08	<0·005
Fish and meat spread	0·6			
Flour confectionery	40·8	25·4	1·04	0·10
Ice cream	6·2	15·0	0·09	0·01
Jellies	1·5	63·5	0·10	0·03
Meat products	43·6			
Milk products	6·5	15·6	0·10	0·02
Pickles and sauces	6·9	37·2	0·26	0·01
Preserves	8·1	38·4	0·31	0·06
Snack foods	7·1			
Soft drinks	215·6	0·7	0·15	<0·005
Total	—	—	4·30	0·88

Appendix IV. Average diet/maximum level of use

Colour: PONCEAU 4R E124

Food 1	Intake of food (g/day) 2	Level of colour in food (mg/kg) 3	Uncorrected intake of colour from food (mg/day; $\frac{\text{Col 2} \times \text{Col 3}}{1000}$) 4	Corrected intake of colour from food (mg/day) 5
Breakfast cereals	12·4			
Butter and margarine	37·2			
Canned fruit	15·2	302·0	4·59	2·26
Canned soup	12·1	9·3	0·11	<0·005
Canned vegetables	31·8			
Cheese	15·3			
Chocolate and sugar confectionery	16·1	250·0	4·03	0·15
Dessert mixes	7·9	775·0	6·12	0·24
Dry mixes (other than dessert mixes)	5·8	340·0	1·97	0·07
Fish and meat spread	0·6			
Flour confectionery	40·8	65·0	2·65	0·25
Ice cream	6·2	150·0	0·93	0·10
Jellies	1·5	336·0	0·50	0·16
Meat products	43·6			
Milk products	6·5	27·0	0·18	0·03
Pickles and sauces	6·9	302·0	2·08	0·06
Preserves	8·1	88·0	0·71	0·14
Snack foods	7·1			
Soft drinks	215·6	8·9	1·92	<0·005
Total	—	—	25·80	3·47

Appendix V. Extreme diet

Colour: PONCEAU 4R E124

Food 1	Intake of food (g/day) 2	Level of colour in food (mg/kg) 3	Uncorrected intake of colour from food (mg/day; $\frac{\text{Col 2} \times \text{Col 3}}{1000}$) 4	Corrected intake of colour from food (mg/day) 5
Breakfast cereals	24·3			
Butter and margarine	72·9			
Canned fruit	29·8	82·3	2·45	1·21
Canned soup	23·7	1·5	0·04	<0·005
Canned vegetables	62·3			
Cheese	30·0			
Chocolate and sugar confectionery	31·6	55·0	1·74	0·07
Dessert mixes	15·5	3·1	0·05	<0·005
Dry mixes (other than dessert mixes)	11·4	13·9	0·16	0·01
Fish and meat spread	1·2			
Flour confectionery	80·0	25·4	2·03	0·19
Ice cream	12·2	15·0	0·18	0·02
Jellies	2·9	63·5	0·18	0·06
Meat products	85·5			
Milk products	12·7	15·6	0·20	0·04
Pickles and sauces	13·5	37·2	0·50	0·02
Preserves	15·9	38·4	0·61	0·12
Snack foods	13·9			
Soft drinks	422·6	0·7	0·30	<0·005
Total	—	—	8·44	1·72

Appendix VI. Child's diet

Colour: PONCEAU 4R E124

Food 1	Intake of food (g/day) 2	Level of colour in food (mg/kg) 3	Uncorrected intake of colour from food (mg/day; $\frac{\text{Col 2 x Col 3}}{1000}$) 4	Corrected intake of colour from food (mg/day) 5
Breakfast cereals	18·6			
Butter and margarine	37·2			
Canned fruit	15·2	82·3	1·25	0·62
Canned soup	12·1	1·5	0·02	<0·005
Canned vegetables	31·8			
Cheese	15·3			
Chocolate and sugar confectionery	35·5	55·0	1·95	0·07
Dessert mixes	11·9	3·1	0·04	<0·005
Dry mixes (other than dessert mixes)	5·8	13·9	0·08	<0·005
Fish and meat spread	0·6			
Flour confectionery	61·2	25·4	1·55	0·15
Ice cream	16·4	15·0	0·25	0·03
Jellies	2·3	63·5	0·15	0·05
Meat products	65·4			
Milk products	6·5	15·6	0·10	0·02
Pickles and sauces	6·9	37·2	0·26	0·01
Preserves	12·2	38·4	0·47	0·09
Snack foods	10·7			
Soft drinks	271·0	0·7	0·19	<0·005
Total	—	—	6·30	1·03

*The insidious and pernicious
promotion of sweeteners
is well orchestrated:
Who is the conductor?*

◇◇◇

Background

Consensus is pretty well established on the need to address the rising levels of obesity with the associated increased risk of health problems. And it makes good, long-term sense to look to improving contributory factors and determinants for our children.

That is where consensus ends.

A key component of the UK Child Obesity Strategy is to "promote diet drinks" through the sugar levy (SDIL – Sugary Drinks Industry Levy. More on this is on the government website, August 2016, under '12 things you should know'). I can find no other official or medical body that is in favour of this strand of the strategy.

Despite strong warnings, fuelled by evidence from across numerous disciplines including gastroenterology, biochemistry, metabolic disease, neuroscience, physiology, genetics and study of the human microbiome, the promotion of artificially sweetened drinks – extending to artificially sweetened foods – continues unabated. (Open discussion has been suppressed, but that is another issue.)

It is not the sugar levy *per se* that is the problem. Nor is it a problem that adults may choose to use sweeteners (here I leave aside *neotame* – concentrated derivative of the sweetener aspartame – and *advantame* – mixture of aspartame and vanillin – which can be used legally without disclosure, therefore no choice).

The problem is the promotion of artificially sweetened products as the healthy option: a promotion that has become more covert and pernicious; a promotion that constantly undermines the education that would promote a healthier, active lifestyle with a healthy, balanced diet at its core.

The time has come to question where the drive to continue with this damaging approach is coming from. Is it largely political, commercial, or a partnership of vested interests that are being put before the public interest? We owe it to our children to investigate.

Early Activity

Back in 2015, before the official launch of the strategy, I noticed an escalation in the use of sweeteners.

But it was in 2016 that the real push started. I thought all that was needed was better education on a more rounded approach, and in September 2016, reluctantly, I came out of 'retirement' and wrote *7 ways of thinking: healthy eating is not just about food*, listing topics to consider in an educational package for schools. Education is paramount in order for this future adult generation to be able to assess the quality of new information and to put it into context.

The drivers do not listen. They determine to pursue this strategy.

One year on, 2017, the promotions of sweeteners were relatively easy to spot. The clues given – for the game *SPOT & STOP the manipulation of choice* – were:

The 'reformulated' products; these likely advertised as *low in sugar, no added sugar, zero sugar, diet, low calorie* or simply *new recipe*. (True reformulation would be great, but that remains more elusive. Usually it is simply replacing sugar with artificial sweeteners.)

The placement of such products to suggest an association with good health.

A clever twist to the original, *Go Well with Shell* advert has returned with *Go Well:* a bottle of clear water in the foreground, diet Coke lined up with a few other 'seemingly' healthy offers to the side. (Unsurprisingly, Coca Cola are particularly strong with the advertising: inexpensive exercise books for children with Coca Cola emblazoned across the top of every page, seen in a retailer for office supplies; their zero sugar/low sugar drink mats adorn many a commercial dining table.)

Price promotions. The Public Health England policy has advocated *Zero Price Promotions on Unhealthy Products*. No dissention on this, except in the crucial definition of healthy and unhealthy.

These were just suggestions to start players off on the game. (Though it was noted that some players had the advantage over consumers: who are the buyers of *neotame* sold on eBay? Where and in what has *neotame* or *advantame* been used?)

Getting More Serious

In December 2017, a publication *Incentives and disincentives for reducing sugar in manufactured foods* was presented by Regional Office for Europe at a joint FAO/WHO symposium on the broader aspects of healthy diets, held in Budapest.

The limitations of the paper, acknowledged by its presenter, are 'skewed towards the UK', and too narrow a focus.

Within the paper, the UK pats itself on the back for its SDIL – but fails to mention the concurrent promotion of diet drinks to children. This is significant, considering The UK then cites *negative public opinion* as a disincentive to reducing the use of sugar, and references a Guardian article as an example of *media reports about negative health impacts of sweeteners*.

Together the two statements infer an ignorant public influenced by uninformed reporting.

I checked out that reference: the Guardian accurately quotes from a study by the University of Adelaide, Australia, presented at the European Association for the study of Diabetes, in Lisbon. The study suggests that the risk of type 2 diabetes might be increased by the use of artificial sweeteners. Responses made by the delegates in Lisbon are reported: the delegates confirm that these findings are in line with previous research. No conclusions can be drawn; more research from across disciplines is needed. (This too is in line with what other scientists say: none claims to have all the answers, but it is increasingly clear that promoting sweeteners is a backward move.)

And still the drivers do not listen. Worse than that, they misrepresent challenges.

The Use and Misuse of the Media and Celebrities

It has long been a tradition to use popular media to convey public health messages. The independent Health Education Authority (HEA), when it existed, had a particularly successful partnership with the 'soaps' – notably the dissemination of information on HIV/AIDS through characters in Eastenders.

Celebrities too may be chosen to convey health messages. Both these methods have been employed.

Misuse

I have not set out to monitor each occasion, but am aware of references, verbal or by a visual suggestion, to Diet Coke or Pepsi on Eastenders, and more so on Coronation Street. Some hit you in the face more strongly than others – and, if it were not for the seriousness of the fall-out, some would be funny because so ludicrous.

Example: Coronation Street. Characters Adam and Eva are taking part in a Christmas community event for children, Adam as an elf, Eva as a fairy. They go behind a curtain to change. We can see just the bare back of Adam as he bends over, eyed by Eva who declares "Oo. I didn't know elves did Diet Coke breaks". (The wall in the booth is adorned with some health/keep fit type posters.)

Example of reference to child obesity: Coronation Street. 'Santa' puts curse on a child. Afterwards says "not sorry, it's what kids are like today. Overweight" Father of child says "Are you calling my daughter fat?" 'Santa' "No, it was the other one".

Just as ludicrous but not funny.

Both these examples came late December 2017, after I had raised a more disturbing issue with ITV about a storyline in Coronation Street. Before I relate something of that correspondence a slight digression is pertinent.

Disagreement in discussions over whether to include fruit juice in the SDIL

From both dietetic and health promotion angles, it beggars belief that anyone could consider taxing the sugar content of fruit or fruit juices. But they did – consider it that is. The use of fruit juice featured quite strongly in the Discussion Paper. Some simply wanted it not to be excluded, others claimed a "distortion of competition". Science and sense prevailed: fruit juice, fruit puree and fruit juice concentrate are excluded from the levy.

Disturbing Misuse: Sour Grapes?

Surely, it could not be because of the refusal to tax the sugar in fruit juice that there is now an insidious effort to dissuade children, or their parents, from choosing fruit/fruit juice. Could it?

Example 1. ITV has been persuaded to run a storyline on Coronation Street in which a baby falls seriously ill each time it has fruit. Characters have repeatedly referred to the baby's "allergy to sugar" (from my own observations, heard earlier and later than the doctor's one appearance, giving a diagnosis of "fructose intolerance" requiring complete avoidance of all fruit and "added sugar").

"Allergy to sugar" does not exist. I sensed where the story might be heading and intervened. Not a complaint: an attempt to forestall any further error of judgment.

These are extracts from my first letter:

... The writer was either thinking of (i) the rare genetic enzyme deficiency that causes an *intolerance of fructose* (sugar in fruit) *or (ii) implications of glycosylated protein ... Any allergic response would be from the protein faction, not the sugar. ... Findings thus far have demonstrated no association between glycosylation and allergic disease in children. ...* (I then gave the journal references.)

All I ask is that you keep the 'messages' simple and unambiguous please. ... Much harder to redress misinformation than it is to expand on the basics.

The reply asserted that viewers would understand characters well enough to know that the regular ones aren't medically knowledgeable, and that they (ITV writers) had taken professional advice from experts on intolerances "of this kind". In other words the regular characters could be excused referring to an "allergy" to sugar or giving any other false information, as they can't be expected to know otherwise.

This approach is particularly insidious **because** viewers, like the regular characters, will not have the required knowledge to know otherwise, or to process all that is going on. (Small point, but dietetic knowledge is more relevant here than medical knowledge. But then viewers will understand that the writers were not knowledgeable in seeking out experts.)

I then wanted clarification on which intolerance ("of this kind"?) they intended to portray. Extracts from that request:

> ... *somewhat reassured ... just so long as the intolerance is the rare hereditary enzyme (aldolase) deficiency ... and the rarity is made clear. If it were fructose malabsorption, often referred generically as intolerance, there would be difficulty in giving a clear message. There are so many variables and so many aspects under research no "expert" has a definitive answer.*

No reply received.

I consider it an error of judgment to introduce such a storyline in the first place, as there is no message to be given that is helpful for the general public. Raising awareness of already known conditions can serve only to cause anxiety and increase the number of worried well attending surgeries. But now that it has been started, I can only hope that the baby is given (dramatically speaking) a **rare** enzyme deficiency.

A failure to clearly distinguish between dietary interventions tailored to suit an individual, and advice appropriate for the general public is irresponsible at best.

Example 2. The BBC programme 'Trust me I'm a Doctor' is not one I watch. However, it came to my attention that there was a slot 'Are we eating too much fruit?', in which relative amounts of sugar in fruits were considered. The short answer is No; we are not eating too much fruit. And it's just silly, totally unnecessary to be thinking about which has the most sugar. Variety is key. The question that should be asked is 'Why was that question posed in the first place?'

Example 3. This is arguably the most serious of the 3 examples because it is on the official NHS website. It comes under 'drink swaps' for children; a short video of a mother describes her shock horror when she learns how much sugar "pure fruit juice" contains. Aghast that pure fruit juice is "marketed as healthy" *(correctly, though suggesting otherwise)* she has learned her lesson to read the label for sugar content. Suggested drink swaps for fruit juice flash up on the screen. And yes, diet drinks are there!

(The focus on calories in the 100 Calorie snack promotion is also questionable. It helps in the promotion of diet drinks, of course, but does not fit in the broader, less prescriptive, food focus model. Suggestions for nutritious snacks, without reference to calories, would be better.)

Accountability:
Opportunity or Provocation?

Could the obvious misuse of the media be an opportunity to bring accountability to the fore? Possibly. But I hesitate.

A quick scan of the workings and structure of Ofcom, (funded by fees from industry and Grant-in-aid from the Government) updated in April 2017, highlights a complicated set-up. Responsibility is spread across several regulatory bodies.

Objections from the examples given above would cut across political propaganda, unfair commercial competition, public interest extending beyond consumer interest and so on. Each aspect dealt with separately, not easy to address as a whole.

(I'm not familiar with competition law – is it all right to mention a product if you don't show it and vice versa, or if you mention more than one product?)

I suspect the drivers of this promotion of diet drinks in favour of fruit juice, are aware of the rules of competition law. I suspect the same would apply to regulation of the other categories, and attention would be paid to abide by them.

Plus, there is an obligation not to disclose details of what has been put forward and discussed in support of the objection, and not to reveal the views of individual Board members. All that may be disclosed is the title of the objection and the subsequent ruling.

If it does not allow for open discussion, perhaps it is better not to rise to the provocation.

> Who is orchestrating these moves?
> Where does the responsibility lie?

We have to go back to the policy "to promote diet drinks" through SDIL as a "key component of the Child Obesity Strategy".

It is a Government policy, so I assume there is a Ministerial responsibility: the person in the relevant Parliamentary position takes guidance from various bodies but ultimately makes the policy decision. It seems no one wants to own, or at least answer the objections to this policy.

Several departments have some involvement: Food Standards Agency (FSA) if it's a safety issue, Department for Environment, Food and Rural Affairs (Defra) if it's an additive issue, Department of Health (DoH) if it's a nutritional issue. The FSA and Defra respond as best they can, but the concerns are complex, across several disciplines: and they are not the policymakers. Ministers pass the buck: divide and rule without responsibility.

There has been too much correspondence to fully catalogue. Perhaps this will suffice:

The Prime Minister's Office, in November 2016, forwarded my letter to Defra, who in turn passed it on to the FSA. (The DoH Ministerial office had earlier established "that this does not fall within the remit of the Department of Health").

Ahead of the Autumn Statement/Budget, 2017, I wrote to the Chancellor on the issues surrounding the SDIL. No reply.

October 2017, I wrote again to the Prime Minister's Office. It was suggested I write to the Minister for Environment, Food and Rural Affairs (currently Michael Gove). I followed the suggestion; no reply.

I copied that October 2017 letter to the Secretary of State for Health (currently Jeremy Hunt). The DoH Ministerial office replied that it was the responsibility of the FSA.

I must be mistaken: I thought the Secretary of State for Health did have a responsibility for policies and the communication of public health messages. But then politics is not my area of expertise.

(Perhaps this spread of responsibility was the template for the updating of Ofcom.)

Notes on other structures that hinder accountability

As stated earlier, the independent HEA no longer exists. Its activities had concentrated on primary health education and promotion; in creating environments that helped prevent ill health; enabling informed, healthy choices. Since its dissolution, to all intents and purposes health education and health promotion have been split and subsumed within other systems.

Health Education (HEE – Health Education England) is under the auspices of NICE (National Institute for the Health & Care Excellence) and health Promotion under FPH (Faculty of Public Health). In both, the focus is on secondary health education and secondary health promotion, which is detecting and treating pre-symptomatic disease; semi-medicalized: effectiveness calculated by measurable changes (for example prevalence of obesity or diabetes) in relation to costs.

But, there is a clear distinction between primary health promotion and secondary health promotion when it comes to guidance on healthy eating. The myriad of contributory factors and determinants that influence the health of an individual, make focus on a single aspect of diet, – be it sugar, or fat, or calorie content – rather than a whole diet approach meaningless.

The discipline of dietetics is the only one with a capability to deliver primary, secondary and tertiary dietary advice to individuals. It is the case (unless changed since I was a State Registered Dietitian) that no specific advice (that is other than that on general, whole diet healthy eating) can be given to an individual without a referral that enables access to that individual's medical notes. This is because it is well established that what is good for one individual can be damaging for another. And that is why a deviance from that mode of practice can result in being struck off the register. Clear accountability.

It is now the position that nutritionists are being employed in surgeries and clinics to give patients advice on healthy eating (hopefully not on individual weight reducing diets). This can be a good thing if simple, general advice on the whole diet is given, as dietitians are in short supply. But it is not a good thing if nutritionists are giving individually tailored, specific advice or if they are echoing the current public health policy of promoting sweeteners as the healthy option. In other words, in an NHS setting, nutritionists will only be as good as the guidelines they are employed to follow.

Ostensibly, the line of accountability within the NHS may appear similar for dietitians and nutritionists, but dietitians will have more opportunity and expertise to disregard blatant errors in official policy when dealing with individuals.

In addition to the established clinical, administrative, managerial pay structures in the NHS, it was thought necessary to introduce a new one, the 'Agenda for Change' pay band. (The first example I am aware of came into force in 2015. They are still being rolled out).

Dietetics comes under the Head of Therapy – which includes several other disciplines – in the Agenda for Change layer. Such positions vary slightly from Trust to Trust but, depending on the grade given, will be expected to play a part in the management of finance and commissioning contracts.

Is this a case of covering all bases?

Insights from personal experience

Firstly, I must emphasize that most people in the NHS, and likely politicians and industry magnates too, are well motivated to do a good job and be successful in both ethical and financial terms. So, it begs the question '*How can such a bad public health policy be implemented*'.

The answer is partly *because* most people are well motivated to do a good job. They are very busy, trust in colleagues and do not want to appear disloyal by causing trouble or disruption to the work in hand: also, because they are focused on the job in hand, are often unaware of the bigger picture.

There are many instances in my career when I could have spoken out, or at least more loudly. I will limit the examples to the period in the early and mid 1990s. Today's situation makes clearer the significance of what was happening back then. So, of relevance.

I am now retired, have no party political allegiance, no dependence on funding, no colleagues relying on my loyalty. I have no restraints whatsoever.

Outline of the most telling post

I refer to the time when I held a newly created post as Health Promotion Service Manager at a large University Hospital Trust. I was based in the Occupational Health Department of an acute hospital. We held several outside contracts, one of which was to provide a health promotion service to the staff at Quarry House, Leeds, home to the Department of Health.

(A clue to the creation of this post came from the existing internal phone directory at Quarry House. It included a name and extension number for a European representative of an American company. A name I recognized as a senior employee in the community sector of the NHS. It was not in the updated directory shortly after my arrival.)

Very enjoyable work, of the type I had done previously in another district, but for that post I was based within a department dedicated to health education and promotion. And, crucially, all the money that we engendered from work with outside companies went straight back into the NHS.

Not so with this advancement in my career.

We had a contract with an American firm that was to act as our consultants on how to attract work from outside. In exchange we, the NHS, paid them a consultancy fee, expenses for travel – I am not sure who paid for our visits to America – and a sizeable portion of our income (not profit, income) from the outside contracts.

The logo of the American company was on printed material we used with clients. (I consider the relationship, in practice, was more of a franchise than consultancy.)

The American 'consultants' made no contribution to the salaries of staff, in spite of much nursing staff time being spent on revising the American promotional material in order to 'better fit' the working practices of our NHS. The Americans then took the said revised promotional material to help secure similar 'consultancy' contracts with additional NHS Trusts in England.

On a ten-day visit to Boston, Massachusetts, to observe the American practice, I found there was no one qualified in health education/promotion and it was not in practice. (I should point out that health promotion proper, is active research. That is, all work is evaluated appropriately and informs the next piece of work.)

This was apparent, not least at the American Health Fairs. All the stands, bar one, were largely concerned with the sale of health insurance. The one exception offered cholesterol testing. Total blood cholesterol was measured and instant results given to the client, though with no attempt at education or explanation. The whole thing was in stark contrast to the health fairs we had been providing for several years, jointly instigated by the HEA and DofH.

The clear injustice is that we were paying the American company when it ought to have been they who were paying the NHS. We were the ones with the expertise and the relevant experience, yet were committed to continue paying heavily for the privilege.

But did I raise hell? No. Other than to grumble, to insist on using the findings of the Kings Fund regarding cholesterol testing, to refuse to spend any time on their promotional material – for which I was hauled over the coals – I just got on with my work. As I said before, it was very enjoyable, well-paid work. And the Americans were pleasant, interesting people.

It was not in my remit to challenge how NHS money was spent, or that of the Department of Health for that matter. (I have no idea how much the additional company – providing a service contracts management team – was paid by Quarry House. The team had no one with health promotion expertise. And as this contract, like the others, was rather non-specific, we came to an informal agreement that I be left alone to just get on with it. But, presumably, they still received their salaries.)

Inside and Outside of the Department of Health contract

There were many instances during this 1990s period when things did not sit comfortably, too many to list. Each, separately, of relative unimportance but considered together have taken me nearer to understanding how a bad public health policy *can* find its way to implementation.

Three brief examples:
- At a district working group meeting, related to smoking, I queried whether the same named person appointed as Chair of a large NHS Trust and Chair

of a company that had a tobacco company as its main sponsor, were one and the same. A visitor from London attended the next meeting. He passed on instructions, quite sternly, that we were to keep quiet because it was all in hand. The conflict would be short-lived. Phew, so that was all right then.
- In November1995 (as a result of my link to DofH) I had sight of and read with interest, the briefing document for the Minister's launch of the new alcohol policy.

The document is a masterclass in how to use words carefully to make a nonsense notion sound reasonable: the new 'Sensible limits' actually suggested a higher weekly total limit – though spread out over days – and that for some people drinking more alcohol would be beneficial to their health. (More on this is in *What did the Government's 1995 message on 'Sensible Drinking' signal?* September, 2016).

There was much opposition to the policy, from both medical bodies and the HEA. Opposition was ridden over roughshod.

N.B. There was always agreement on the advice to think in terms of daily alcohol limits rather than weekly. Obviously, the advice should never have been to increase levels of drinking.

- I was invited to a focus group meeting, to consider the standard of the journal for health promotion specialists. At the close, I spoke briefly with the two facilitators from HEA. They were upset, reluctant to say much – "we might be losing our jobs" – but did confide that someone (I gathered from either Government or Civil Service but they didn't name anyone) frequently came to their office and checked over what they were writing. I was told that they were under pressure to word articles in a way that 'evidenced' health policies were being successful.

Enough is Enough

The 1990s are past, in time but not in practice.

A news bulletin last week filmed children in a gym: the voice-over boasted of the facilities being provided from the sugar levy revenue. Apparently, we have a world-leading strategy for tackling childhood obesity.

Oh, come on!

Yes, it's lovely to provide fun opportunities for our children to take more exercise. The leisure centre in my town is council owned. It is an excellent new building that houses swimming pool, gym and bowling alley. I don't want to gripe, but doesn't the wall that sports a full mural advert for Coca Cola dilute the message somewhat. If you miss the wall, not to worry, there is always the drinks machine in the lobby and the drinks cabinet in the café.

Is this what is known as a tax benefit?

As regards the "world-leading" aspect, my reading of the situation is that the implementation of the sweeteners promotion is of interest, but not in a positive way. There are concerns that the UK is setting a bad example by taking the 'quick, easy, cheap' route, in promoting sweeteners as the healthy option and a key way of addressing childhood obesity. Others, in the UK and internationally, accept that research suggests otherwise on both counts.

Over the years (since 2011 when I attempted to find answers regarding the non-declaration of *neotame*) I have steered away from politics and commercial machinations – the patent expiring for *aspartame*, production becoming cheaper in China than Japan, the need for new innovations etcetera. And even now, I do not want to become embroiled in such things more than I have to.

But the August 2016 statement was a dire warning that the forces at play, the 'drivers', meant to ignore the sound scientific research that had been put before them. The EFSA review of safety of sweeteners, 2013, limited in scope, is the basis for the mantras that attempt to justify the unjustifiable.

The consequences of this irresponsible health policy are more far reaching than the abuses of power and influence that took place before. Ultimately, adults will choose for themselves how much alcohol to drink or whether to smoke.

In the current scenario, both children and adults are being denied choice.

(Incidentally, the shift to referring to calorie content approach, achieves nothing in mitigation, only in masking the intentions.)

The ways in which choice – to avoid sweeteners – is being denied are at least threefold.

1. Non-declaration of neotame and advantame. This needs a few words of clarification:

It is not being suggested that any law is being broken in using *neotame* or *advantame* and not putting it on the food label. They both share the same active ingredient as the sweetener *aspartame*, but may be used and classed in a different way. If they are used under an additive classification – either a sweetener or a flavour enhancer – they will be declared on the label. However, there are times when they can be used and classed differently – for example, as a processing aid. There is then no legal requirement to declare their use.

Hence, consumers cannot exercise their right to avoid them, if that is their choice.

This policy aggravates that situation: it gives the green light to use *neotame* and *advantame* more frequently. How much we might be consuming is an unknown quantity.

2. Choice of non-artificially sweetened foods and drinks is unfairly restricted for the poorest families under 'zero price promotions' on sugary products, as advocated in the Public Health Report of January 2017.

3. Procurement contracts in schools are expected to use Government Buying Standards: the use of *aspartame, neotame* and *advantame* currently falls within their strategy for reducing sugar.

And now, the same applies to procurement in hospitals. NHS England has released, January 2018, an updated contract for hospitals, which for the first time includes a clause prohibiting the sale of sugar sweetened beverages.

I repeat, enough is enough. Yes, we want to reduce sugar consumption. But children, and consumers generally, have the right not to be force-fed sweeteners.

Summary of where we are now

There remains a refusal to accept a right to choose. There remains a refusal to move from a "proven safe" mantra, when it is clear that lack of evidence of harm does not equate to evidence of safety. The advice lags behind research.

There is an increased separation between those appointed to implement the policy and those with the scientific expertise.

Our increased knowledge of interrelated metabolic and neurological pathways and associated regulators, tells us repeatedly that there is much more still to learn. It leads us to question what we have previously accepted as "safe". The new knowledge comes from across many disciplines. Perhaps this is one of the reasons the policymakers missed the implications of the findings.

Many manufacturers and retailers recognize the need to work in partnership and are willing to do so.

As a help to those consumers who want to avoid certain things, three supermarkets have welcomed an opportunity to assert that neither *aspartame, neotame* nor *advantame* are used in the production of their **own-label** products: these are *bySainsbury's, M&S, Co-op.*

Professor of Retailing at Manchester University, Peter McGoldrick, is to be congratulated on an award of £25million for the foundation of the Tesco Sustainable Consumption Institute.

This is an abstract from his work, part of Retail Forum Studies to 'investigate retail/manufacturer roles in promotion of healthier eating patterns':

We propose that marketers should undertake health promotion activities as part of their Corporate Social Responsibility (CSR) practices, thus benefitting consumers, public health, corporate reputations, shareholder value, and alignment with public policy priorities.

A Better Way Forward

It has to start with more openness. Closely followed by a change in direction away from promoting sweeteners and to giving messages that encompass the diet as a whole. It is a suboptimal whole diet that is the leading risk factor for death and disability. Tinkering with one element this year and another the next, based on data subject to various interpretations gets us nowhere fast.

A clear, unambiguous policy will be easier to promote, easier to work together on. But, importantly, of all the stakeholder interests, public health has to be the main priority.

If Professor McGoldrick's words are to be heeded (and why should they not, they are valuable words indeed) then we had better make sure that the 'corporate marketers' have a good understanding of what **health** promotion really is: a return to the ethos of primary health promotion (and a reminder that the majority of the population is not obese) – the enabling of **informed** healthy **choices** to be made. Food manufacturers and retailers are not pharmacists; food is an enjoyment not a prescription.

This is not just rhetoric: giving clear information and then allowing choice, yields the better benefits long-term. Study of health behaviour is an integral part of health promotion.

The UK's Eat well Guide, illustrated with a 'healthy plate' is an excellent start, and one already familiar to many. It's a visual way of expressing the relative proportions of foods from the main food groups. It is simpler to think in terms of proportions by volume than by calories, and preferable for many reasons.

Keeping that simple balance, and choosing a variety of foods from within those groups will provide a healthy diet. This simple, basic message goes a long way. (Weight control is largely by adjusting portion size, keeping the same balance.)

I would like to see a poster displayed in supermarkets. The plate replaced by a basket, with no additional, written information. One third filled with a variety of fruit & vegetables, one third with a variety of carbohydrate rich foods and one third with a variety of protein rich foods: neither dairy nor fats in a section of their own. Posters of baskets in shops: the 'healthy plate' illustration, with additional information, to continue to be widely available.

The French agency ANSES advocates more dairy products, beans and lentils, and less meat than does the UK. Not a problem. No need to bicker. The difference serves to demonstrate that there is plenty of scope for individual choice.

We should guide not dictate. We can then expect less resistance to making healthier changes.

Education for our children: giving them the edge.

Education in the (many) sciences related to food and diet should begin early in schools. The more that is taught and learned, the less will be the influence of biased or misleading information. (I still come across people who think of cholesterol as a type of fat!)

Possibly not the preferred method for all teachers, but my preference is for introducing the periodic table – the alphabet of the language of science – as soon as possible. And to relate the foods to elements – carbohydrates, fats, alcohol and proteins all compounds of the same elements: these are carbon, hydrogen and oxygen. (Protein also has nitrogen, which allows protein to have additional uses.)

The elements are the same; it's the proportions of the elements that make a difference, just as the proportions of ingredients can make different cakes (or something more healthy).

It is but a small step to relate the balance of foods, expressed on the healthy plate, to the balance our bodies try to maintain (homeostasis). If we have a lot of one thing our bodies will try to convert it to another. Micronutrients (fruit and vegetables are rich sources) help trigger and regulate the conversions:

Fat (saturated fatty acids) converts to cholesterol (a sugar, alcohol compound)
Sugar converts to fat
Alcohol converts to triglyceride (3 fatty acids, 1 glycerol – a sugar)

It follows that if we eat a balanced diet, our bodies do not have to work quite so hard to achieve that inner balance.

(The more advanced pupil will be able to compare homeostasis with la Chatalier's principle in chemistry, and to appreciate that what happens in vitro may not happen in vivo.)

It is another small step to understand that the so-called good cholesterol and so-called bad cholesterol is actually the same cholesterol: the same (sugar, alcohol) compound but travelling around the body together with different proportions of fatty acids and proteins (in the form of lipoproteins). The different proportions affect the speed the lipoproteins travel. The slower ones might get left behind in the arteries.

(Here, the more advanced pupil can relate to the higher density of protein, polarity, to the electrical currents in physics, progress to the gut-brain axis, neuroscience, and artificial intelligence.)

Level of simplification will vary, and that is only one approach that can be used, of course. But we do need to find ways to engage with children to have a broader understanding of healthy eating and healthy lifestyles in general.

There is more wonder in the complexities of life when there is less ignorance.

Conclusion

So, who is the conductor of this well orchestrated promotion of sweeteners? Is it an arrogant bullyboy, hiding in the wings whilst the sections of his orchestra each make unpleasant sounds under his, so discreet, direction? We don't know. Accountability is blurred.

We do know, we have seen, that it is perfectly possible for health policies not in the public interest, to be pushed through.

We do know that the repercussions from this policy are set to worsen if action is not taken, if contracts are not scrutinized.

Sound policy must be established for the UK quickly, because until it is we are vulnerable to contracts (or trade deals) favouring suppliers of re-formulated foods – of the current, sugar replaced with sweeteners type, not truly re-formulated. Schools and hospitals are under immediate threat in this respect.

It is not necessary to identify individuals who champion the promotion of sweeteners. What matters is that the Government now changes its approach, works with public bodies, manufacturers and retailers in a constructive way that genuinely helps the whole population to have a healthy diet and a healthy lifestyle.

January 2018.

Articles referred to in this essay can be accessed through this link: https:// www.linkedin.com / today / posts / pamela-theophilus-gardner-71557180

Appendix: About Phenylalanine

Four basic facts:

1. Phenylalanine is an amino acid, one of the building blocks of protein.
2. It is 'essential', meaning that the body cannot make it so it has to be obtained in food.
3. It is used in the body to make tyrosine – and in the formation of some neurotransmitters such as dopamine.
4. It is harmful for those with the genetic condition phenylketonuria (PKU), characterized by a deficiency in the enzyme phenylalanine hydroxylase. Approximately 1 in 10,000 of the population has PKU.

It is important to know that phenylalanine **never** occurs 'naturally' on its own in food: it is widely and easily available in protein foods, but **always** as part of a protein, never an isolate.

We know, from *untreated PKU*, that when unusually high levels of phenylalanine cross the blood-brain barrier there is substantial damage to the development and function of the brain. This causes severe mental retardation, and damage to the central nervous system.

To avoid those consequences, each baby is tested at birth for the condition so that, if positive, dietary control of phenylalanine can be instigated quickly and control maintained throughout its growth (and, if female, also during pregnancy). A developing brain is at the greatest risk, but later research suggests it may be beneficial to maintain some control throughout adulthood.

In addition to classic PKU there are variants of PKU (terms vary), involving deficiency of co-factors rather than the enzyme, which also result in raised phenylalanine levels. It is significant in the context of reducing risks of diabetes, that one such deficiency is associated with a risk for Maturity Onset Diabetes of the Young (MODY). Intellectual disability is one of the common findings in variants of PKU as in classic PKU.

It is undisputed that the effects of phenylalanine in untreated PKU are causal. But the **precise** mechanism by which the damage is caused has not yet been fully elucidated.

Until the precise mechanism is known, we do not have enough information to properly determine the consequences of ingesting phenylalanine as an isolate – not as an integral part of a protein – in food or drink.

This is the basis for concern about the use of phenylalanine in sweeteners, flavour enhancers, or undisclosed as in the case of processing aids, for example.

Phenylalanine is the active ingredient in *aspartame*, *neotame* – a concentrated derivative of *aspartame*, and *advantame* – a mixture of *aspartame* and vanillin.

No Ifs, Ands, or Buts

◇◇◇

Back in the day, the 1960s to be precise, when I started my first job as a 'rater' (someone who assesses claims) in the then *Ministry of Pensions and National Insurance*, armed with pen and paper, I enjoyed the connection I had with actual people.

A 'yes' or a 'no' answer to particular questions on a claim form might warrant an interview to clarify the specific situation, before consulting the massive tomes – known as Codes – to establish entitlement or disallowance. There was the challenge of ifs and buts; the flicking backwards and forwards through the pages of the Codes; the satisfaction of eventually finding the solution.

Much later – a family and an education later – I became a state registered dietitian. In clinics I met the new challenge of the '*Yes but'ters*' (no, nothing to do with eating butter): these were the, mercifully few, patients who responded to every suggestion with a "Yes, but …"; "Yes, but I can't …"; "Yes, but that won't work for me …". Invariably they had been referred under protest; they had sought help for a medical condition and resented any inference that changes to diet could have an influence; admittance to such a notion might imply their habits had contributed to their current state. Generally, once they had had their say – put forward an unrequired defence with a string of "Yes (I knew that) but …" mitigations – there was a turn around and co-operation.

When I moved into health education and promotion, 'ifs and buts' (including the odd variation – spliffs and butts) abounded, under the grander terminology of, for example, inhibitory and facilitating factors in the psychology of health behaviour.

It was after I retired and volunteered at a Citizens Advice Bureau (CAB) that, most surprisingly, I was thrown back to those early years of employment – checking rules and conditions of entitlement to various benefits: the difference being (apart from the obvious one of not being an employee of any benefit agency) that the information was on computer, not in physical tomes.

There was another anomaly worth a mention: it was the staff in the actual benefit offices who had suggested to some of their claimants, or potential claimants, that they seek advice from the CAB in order to first get an idea of entitlement. It seems that those civil servants were no longer trained in the intricacies of regulations. They made assessments by simply keying in the responses on claim forms, and the computer programmes supplied the yeah or nay. Unfortunately, the said programmes did not have the capacity to handle all the 'ifs and buts': the nuances of circumstance.

Some questions, on these and other types of forms we have to fill in on occasions, may ask us to expand on an answer … *If yes, give details* … but often it's the case of giving a best fit 'yes' or 'no' answer. Where are those 'Yes, but …' or No, but …' opportunities when you need them?

This diminished level of communication applies to other modes of interaction: the brief, abrupt, shortened to almost a coded language of texts and twitter comments, gives more scope for ambiguity; makes it more difficult to express wants and emotions; causes more frustration.

Perhaps extra icons that signify a need to qualify what we have just said (*if, and, but* icons) would be useful adjuncts to the smiley face and other available emoticons.

Conversely, we have an increase in the level of Information Communication technology (ICT). The Artificial Intelligence (AI), used in both ICT and robot technology, is an important advancement that has the potential to address a range of problems, whether of a health, social or economic nature.

But, use of stark, big data without good data processing algorithms – proper integration of all ifs, ands, and buts – does not provide correct answers.

'No ifs, ands, or buts' phrase dates back, in some form or other, to at least the 17th century. It has an inference of certainty, no doubts or excuses.

In science, we find that the more we learn the greater the realization that there are many more unknowns; there are few certainties, few absolutes.

Good healthcare is particularly reliant on good communication, between patient and physician, between disciplines, and in the conveyance of global health messages. Interestingly, the ability of a patient to repeat this centuries old phrase has been used in recent times by neurologists to test for cognitive impairment.

There is a level of irony here: artificial intelligence assessed by the quality of its algorithms; human intelligence assessed by an ability to repeat the opposite of a good algorithm.

Matador

For exclusive discounts on Matador titles,
sign up to our occasional newsletter at
troubador.co.uk/bookshop